Acclaim for *Childhood*

"This is not the book of the year, but the book of this damned century. *Childhood* is going to reach everyone and go on reaching people for generations to come."
—Allan Sillitoe, author of
*The Loneliness of the
Long-Distance Runner*

"Deserves to be widely read."
—*The New York Times Book Review*

"Simple . . . terse . . . shattering."
—Harold Pinter, winner of the
Nobel Prize in Literature

"A dark fairy tale . . . of the fears and anguish of a child, based on experiences that could not be grasped by reason, irrational yet truly real."
—Heinrich Böll, winner of the
Nobel Prize in Literature

"This is a book that matters. There is a purity in it which leaves you speechless, a humanity which gives you no rest."
—*Die Zeit*

"A child sees the barbarities of an event such as the Holocaust not in terms of race and politics, but in the way a Martian would see them, as amazing and stupefying instances of the cruelty of man. Jona Oberski conveys this amazement in an unembroidered and memorable way."
—Thomas Keneally,
author of *Schindler's List*

PENGUIN CLASSICS

CHILDHOOD

JONA OBERSKI was born in 1938 in Amsterdam. His experiences in the Bergen-Belsen concentration camp during World War Two formed the basis for his classic novel *Childhood*, which was made into a movie and translated into twenty languages. Oberski published several more novels, but for most of his professional career he worked as a nuclear and particle physicist. He lives in Amsterdam.

RALPH MANHEIM (1907–1992) was one of the foremost translators of his generation. He was awarded the National Book Award in Translation and a MacArthur Fellowship. The PEN/Ralph Manheim Medal for Translation is named for him.

JIM SHEPARD is the author of *The Book of Aron*, a novel narrated by a child in a Warsaw Ghetto orphanage, as well as several other novels and collections of short stories, including *Like You'd Understand, Anyway*, which won the Story Prize and was a finalist for the National Book Award, and *Project X*, which won the Massachusetts Book Award. His work has appeared in *The New Yorker*, *The Paris Review*, *The Atlantic*, *Granta*, and *Harper's Magazine*. Shepard teaches at Williams College in Williamstown, Massachusetts.

JONA OBERSKI

Childhood

Translated by
RALPH MANHEIM

Afterword by
JIM SHEPARD

PENGUIN BOOKS

PENGUIN BOOKS
Published by the Penguin Group
Penguin Group (USA) LLC
375 Hudson Street
New York, New York 10014

USA | Canada | UK | Ireland | Australia | New Zealand | India | South Africa | China
penguin.com
A Penguin Random House Company

First published in the United States of America by Doubleday & Company, Inc. 1983
This edition with an afterword by Jim Shepard published in Penguin Books 2014
Published by arrangement with Doubleday, an imprint of The Knopf Doubleday
Publishing Group, a division of Random House LLC

Copyright © 1978 by Jona Oberski
English translation copyright © 1983 by Doubleday & Company, Inc., Hodder & Stoughton,
Ltd. and Lester Orpen Dennys, Ltd.
Afterword copyright © 2014 by Jim Shepard

Originally published in Dutch as *Kinderjaren* by Uitgeverij BZZToH, Den Haag.

LIBRARY OF CONGRESS CATALOGING-IN-PUBLICATION DATA
Oberski, Jona, 1938–
[Kinderjaren. English]
Childhood / Jona Oberski ; translated by Ralph Manheim ; afterword by Jim Shepard.
pages cm. — (Penguin classics)
ISBN 978-0-14-310741-5
1. Bergen-Belsen (Concentration camp)—Fiction. 2. Holocaust, Jewish (1939–1945)—
Netherlands—Fiction. I. Manheim, Ralph, 1907–1992, translator. II. Title.
PT5881.25.B39K5613 2014
839.313'64—dc23
2014018007

Printed in the United States of America
1 3 5 7 9 10 8 6 4 2

This is a work of fiction based on real events.

For my foster parents,
who had quite a time
with me.

Amsterdam, 19 November 1977, 7 P.M.

grass in a blue teapot
set apart, amongst the growing,
fading, still living grass.

JUDITH HERZBERG
From *Beemdgras en zachte dravik*
(Meadow grass and soft brome)

Contents

Contents

Childhood

Childhood

MISTAKE

"Don't be afraid. Everything's all right. I'm right here."

The hand on my cheek was my mother's; her face was close to mine. I could hardly see her. She whispered and stroked my hair. It was dark. The walls were wood. There was a funny smell. It sounded like there were other people there. My mother lifted my head up and pushed her arm under it. She hugged me and kissed me on the cheek.

I asked her where my father was.

"There's been a mistake, but everything will be all right. We've gone away for a few days with a lot of other people, but we'll be going home soon and Daddy will be there too. They've made a mistake, so we'll have to stay here for a few days, visiting the way we visited with Trude a while ago. Remember? Trude made cauliflower. But when it was on your plate you wouldn't eat it, because you weren't used to cauliflower. She tried to make you believe that babies come out of cauliflowers. But you know they come out of their mothers' tummies. You came out of mine. Remember those pictures at home that show you coming out of my tummy and drinking milk from my breast, and having a bath. Remember?

"Daddy had to go to the office yesterday morning. Then they came to get us, but you were very sleepy. Remember? We walked a long way. I left a note for Daddy, because they made a mistake, we really didn't have to go. They'll give Daddy the note and in a few days we'll be going home again. There are lots of people here with children, so you won't be bored. We haven't got many toys because we had to leave in a hurry. I couldn't even tell the woman next door. Later on, we were lucky enough to meet some people we knew. Remember? That nice Mr. L. joked with you. He promised to let Daddy know. He must have told him long ago. Maybe when it gets light tomorrow there'll be a letter from Daddy.

"There are other people here, that's why we have to whisper. Otherwise, we'd wake them up, and all the people here are tired. You're tired too. You slept the whole time in the train. Remember the train? No, angel, maybe not. You were too sleepy.

"It's too bad they made this mistake. But we'll be home again in a few days."

Somebody shouted shhh. My mother whispered so close to my ear that it tickled. "Go to sleep now. I'm right here, I won't go away. Tomorrow we'll take a look at our camp, and in a few days we'll go home to Daddy."

She gave me a kiss. The air in my nose was cold. It was cold under the blankets too. I cuddled up to my mother and her warm breath blew into my nose.

On the second day a letter came from my father, and on the fourth day there was a package. Every day I asked if we could go home. But she said no, it would be a few days.

A week later we went home. A few other people went, but most stayed.

My father was waiting for us.

He kissed my mother and me and they cried.

JUMPING JACK

"You're good at keeping your eyes shut," my mother said. "Shut them good and tight. I'm going to carry you inside, and you can open them when I tell you. All right?"

I shut my eyes. Through my closed eyelids I could see the light in my room. I heard my father. "Can we come in?" my mother called. She picked me up in her arms. I looked to see what was happening. "No, angel," she said. "Shut them tight. You promised." She carried me through the house. My eyes kept wanting to open, so I put my hand over them. I noticed we'd come to where my father was. "You can open them now." In that same moment my father and mother began to sing "Happy Birthday to You." My father and mother kissed me on the cheeks and I kissed them back. My father took me from my mother's arms. My mother looked at me. I saw the lamp reflected in her dark eyes. I felt my father's rough cheek and tickly hair on my cheek. His hair was black. My mother's hair was red. We were wearing our dressing gowns. My father's was light brown. My mother's was light blue. There were all sorts of different-colored things on the table.

"Aren't you going to unwrap your presents?"

I looked at my father. The colors of the things on the table were reflected in his eyes. I gave him a kiss on the nose. That made him laugh.

"Don't you want to see your presents?" He wanted to put me on the floor, but I was so comfortable just the way I was. I had one arm around his neck and I held him tight.

"All this is for you." My mother smiled at me and pointed at the table and kissed me. She picked up a red package, began to open it, and asked me to help her. While she held the package, I tried to get the paper off with one hand. It tore.

"It doesn't matter, it's only the paper." My father put me down on the floor and I pulled the paper off with both hands. Out came a flat wooden doll with strings. He was brown and red and yellow with a laughing face. My mother took hold of a string and held it up. "Here, pull this." I held on to my father's dressing gown with one hand and pulled the string with the other. My mother helped me. The jumping jack spread his arms and legs when I pulled and dropped them when I let go.

"We'll hang him up over your bed. Here, angel, hold him in both hands." I took him. I had fun with my toy. My father had his arm around my mother's shoulder, and all together we watched the jumping jack. I had to laugh every time he spread his legs. They laughed too.

"There are lots of other presents. Look." I looked at the jumping jack in my hand.

"It's too much at once," my father said. "Let's give him the rest later." He grabbed me around the waist with his two big hands. He lifted me up and I flew through the air. He set me down on his shoulders, bent low to get through the doors, and plopped me down on my parents' big bed. I crawled under the light-blue blankets. My father and mother drank tea in bed. We laughed at my jumping jack.

They gave me the rest of the presents later.

SHOPKEEPER

The door of the shop was behind my back. It was open and my mother was inside. I could hear her talking with the shopkeeper. The rain was coming down on my hood. My hands under my cape kept dry. I put one hand through the slit. I saw the raindrops coming down on my hand. The drops kept giving me little cold taps, each time in a different place.

There was sand all around me. I took a light-yellow brick and put it down on end in the dark-yellow sand. I let go. It fell over. I smoothed the sand a little with the brick. Then it stayed up.

My mother came and stood near me. "Isn't it nice in the rain? Do you want your pail and shovel? I'll get them for you." I looked around. There was no one in sight. All I could see was the shop: a wet window and a dark hole. My mother called out to the shopkeeper. She said I was playing outside the door. The shopkeeper called back, "All right." I looked after her. The shopkeeper came and stood in the doorway. "Nice rain, eh?" I pointed at my mother. "She'll be right back," he said. My mother tapped hard on the windowpane and waved to me. I laughed and waved back. I took another brick and stood it on end. It fell over every time I let go. Suddenly my mother was standing beside me. She shoveled sand into the pail. "You see?" she said. "This is how it's done." I knew that already. I started shoveling. "I'm going back up again," she said, and kissed me on my wet forehead. I gave her a kiss on her wet chin.

With my shovel I beat the sand flat. The bricks stayed up. My mother had brought a mold too. I put sand in the mold and made a row of sand pies.

_____

The bricks fell over. I saw two feet. I stood up. A boy was look-ing at me. He lifted one foot and brought it down on a sand pie. I looked at the sand pies. Bam. The biggest one was squashed. He stamped on every one of them. The mold disappeared in the sand. "Ha ha ha," he went and ran away. I had to laugh too. I took my shovel and dug the mold out of the sand. I made new pies on a flat stretch of sand. I filled the pail, I thought I'd make a big sand pie. I smoothed out a place with my hand. The feet almost stepped on my hands. I moved them away quickly and looked up at the boy. He stamped on all my pies. He shouted "Ha ha" and "Great" and "This is fun." I looked at our win-dow. My mother wasn't there. The shop door was closed. My hood got pulled off my head. "Ha ha, what a crazy Jewish coat." A lot of sand came down on my head. I began to cry. The pail fell on the ground beside me. I stood up. I ran to our house. I ran up the stairs. I banged on the door. My mother opened it. She picked me up. "Angel," she said. "What is it?" She hugged me tight. She wiped the sand off my face with a washcloth. She kissed me and brushed the sand out of my hair. I stopped cry-ing. "Oh, what a deep sigh," she said. She took me over to the window. "Haven't you brought your pail and shovel back?"

She went and got them. I didn't want to go with her. I looked out of the window. She came back. I ran to the door to meet her and asked if she had the mold too. She went back, but she couldn't find the mold.

Later my father came home. We told him what had hap-pened. My father asked if it was the grocer's son. I nodded. My father went out. I looked out of the window and saw him going into the shop. After a while he came back. He took me on his lap and kissed me. The grocer said it couldn't have been his son; he said he'd always sold us everything we wanted, which had got him into plenty of trouble, and my mother shouldn't have left me outside the shop all by myself. My father told my mother never to do it again.

My mother was crying when she came home next day. My father comforted her. She said, "He wouldn't sell me anything.

I asked him why, seeing we've always paid promptly. He said it was forbidden." My father said my mother could go to the shop that belonged to someone we knew, who'd be glad to help us. My mother said it was a long way to go, but all right.

I climbed up on my mother's lap. I put my arm around her neck. She hugged me tight. My father came over to us.

"We'll make a circle of heads," he said. "That way we can give each other a kiss all at once."

That's just what we did.

WINDOW WASHER

"The window washer is here." My mother woke me gently from my afternoon nap. "Would you like to watch him?"

I stood up and threw my arms around her neck. She carried me into the parlor. The tile stove was burning and the lamp was lit. I heard music.

I climbed up on the bench across from the bookcase. The window washer waved at me through the window. I waved back. My mother brought me a cup of hot milk. It was dark outside. The window washer was dressed in white. He wet the windows with a sponge and rubbed from top to bottom and from left to right to left. Now and then he'd scratch the pane with his fingernail. Then he did the same thing with another sponge that he dipped in a different pail. He pressed the wet sponge flat against the glass. Streams of water zigzagged down the pane. He wiped away most of the water with his black wiper—right, left, right in big circles. He took a chamois out of his white pail, squeezed it out and folded it. Left, right, left, same as with the wiper, but this time it was harder. I heard it squeaking on the glass. My mother looked up from her ironing board. She turned the music louder. "Do you like this music?" I nodded. She began to sing. "It's Mozart. That's the name of the composer. Remember that name, Mozart."

She put the iron down on its end and took something from the pile of clothes. "Would you dampen it for me?" she asked. I took another swallow of hot milk. Then I went over to her. She dipped my hand in the lukewarm water and sprinkled the dress she was going to iron. The window washer pursed his lips and nodded. He stood on the edge of the window frame, moved the ladder and wet the other window. My mother rolled up the dress. I dipped my hand in the water again, sprinkled some other things and rolled them up. Then I sprinkled my hair.

I went to my room, climbed up on my bed, and took my jumping jack. I made it dance for the window washer. He clapped his hands. Then he climbed down the ladder.

My mother took me on her lap. She gently brushed my hair, to the left on one side, to the right on the other.

"See what a pretty boy you are, what beautiful curls." She leaned to one side and looked at me. I looked at her. "Look in the mirror." I looked at the window and saw us sitting there. My mother's face was right next to mine. I could also see the lamp and the white cover of the ironing board clearly.

THE FERRY

My mother buttoned my cape and put my hood over my head. She pulled my hands out through the slits and put my mittens on. She kissed me and I gave my father my hand. Together we went down the stone front steps and out into the street. We went down the street a short way through the snow, crossed a small empty lot, and came to the Amstel ferry landing. It was a windy day and the waves splashed against the dark-brown wood.

The ferry was on the other side. I was shivering. My father stretched out his arms and slapped his sides. He stamped his feet fast at the same time. I did the same. He gave me his hand and we both kept stamping until the ferry landed and we went on board.

"Well," the ferryman asked me, "do you still want to be a ferryman?" I nodded. All three of us went to the pilothouse together. The ferryman climbed the stairs. "How about it?" he called down. "You coming up? It's time to push off."

I looked at my father. My father said to the ferryman, "It's impossible. The pilothouse is too small. What if someone sees us?"

"Heck, there's no one else on board."

My father took me up the stairs. The door opened and I went in. There wasn't enough room for my father. Through the window in the door I saw his head going down slowly. I looked at the ferryman. He lifted me up and held my head to the window. My father was standing at the foot of the stairs. He waved to me. I laughed. The ferryman put me down. "We're pushing off." He turned a lot of handles and pulled a chain. The whistle scared me. There was a big steering wheel in front of me. "Take the wheel," he said to me. "If you turn it like this, we'll go this way; and like this, we'll go that way."

There was such a racket I could hardly understand what he was saying. Everything was creaking and pounding, and the engine was making a terrible noise too. When the whole boat shook I knew we had left the shore. The ferryman took my hands and put them on the wheel. I looked around. "Oh," he said. "Naturally you can't see anything." He lifted me up with one hand. It was no fun being lifted like that. My father was down below, looking at the water. His hair was blowing all over his face. We were in the middle of the river. I saw the waves. I grabbed the steering wheel and turned it. "Now look what you've done," said the ferryman. "We're going the wrong way." I saw we weren't heading for the opposite shore, we were going down the river. "Turn her back, captain," he sang out with a laugh. I turned the wheel back with all my might and then we were heading the right way again. The ferryman put me down and laughed. "You're a fine little skipper all right." I grabbed the steering wheel and tried to turn it again. But it wouldn't budge. "Let go now, we're going to dock." The ferryman turned the wheel fast. I looked at him but he didn't lift me up. When the boat stopped moving, he took me down the stairs.

My father took a cigar from his inside pocket. "Give it to the ferryman. For letting you steer."

I looked at my father. My cape was blowing every which way. There were black spots on the yellow material. "Hey, look at that," said my father. "Oh well, that's what it's like to steer a boat."

I gave the ferryman the cigar. "Thank you kindly. Are you coming back this way?" As we were leaving the ferry, he said to my father, "The little fellow did a good job. And he already speaks good Dutch."

My father said, "He was born here. We do our best to speak Dutch with him."

"Back so soon?" said my mother when we came in.

"The ferryman let him steer the boat and he didn't want to go for a walk."

"Was the ferryman pleased with the cigar?"

"Yes, he was delighted. He's a nice man. If only they were all like that," said my father. He also said my cape had got some spots of oil on it and he cleaned them off.

My mother took my hands in hers. Mine were cold, hers were warm. My fingers tingled.

MR. PAUL

My father took me with him to his office. My mother had sewn a yellow star on my coat. She said, "Look, now you've got a pretty star, just like Daddy." I thought the star was pretty, but I'd rather have gone without. We had a long way to go. Luckily my father lifted me up on his shoulders now and then.

When we got there, I saw a plain front door just like at our house. I asked if I could ring, but my father said he'd rather do it himself. He rang the bell a lot of times. I asked why he did that because I was never allowed to give more than one quick ring. He said he'd tell me later. We went up the wooden stairs and down a dark hallway. Then he knocked at a door. Someone opened and said good morning to my father in a soft voice. Then he said to me, "So you're your father's son. Glad to meet you, sir." And he gave me his hand. I laughed kind of, and my father told me to say good day to Mr. Paul. Then my father showed me his place. It was a little table with a typewriter on it. Then he said he had to get something in another room. He said I could sit in his place or walk around, but I mustn't touch anything. He showed me which room he was going to.

On each side of my father's table there was another little table with a typewriter on it. And more next to them. And in front of me and behind me too. I went over to Mr. Paul and asked him what all the typewriters were for. He said they were for typing and asked me if I'd counted them. I started counting. I went up and down the aisles and counted up to thirty. That was right. Mr. Paul asked if I'd like to type something. I looked at him to see if he'd really let me. He picked me up on his lap and put a fresh sheet of paper in the machine. He showed me how it worked and explained exactly what he was doing. He took hold of my finger. We typed my name together, and then he turned the roller so I could read it.

"Is it fun?" I wanted to type some more. He took some cushions, piled them up on my father's chair and sat me down on top of them. That way I could reach the keys.

I started typing, and he went back to typing on his own machine. I tried to type my father's name, but I had trouble finding the right letters. They were all mixed up and they looked different from the ones I'd learned in kindergarten. When I couldn't find a letter, Mr. Paul let me ask him for help. He'd show me the letter on his machine, and then I'd go back, climb up on my pile of cushions and type it on my paper. After a while I'd had enough. Mr. Paul had stopped too. He was still rustling papers, but otherwise it was still in the room. The white paper hurt my eyes. The keys of the typewriter sparkled.

My father came back and saw I'd been typing. "That was very kind of you, Mr. Paul," he said.

Then we left. I gave Mr. Paul my hand. He asked if he could keep my hand, but I shook my head. I asked my father if we could take a typewriter home with us. My father said no, we couldn't. But it was all right to take my paper.

When we got home, I showed it to my mother and I told her about the white light without any lampshades and about all the typewriters and Mr. Paul.

MUIDERPOORT

A man was shouting. I woke up. The door of my room was pulled open. Somebody stomped in. The light went on. "What's in here?" the man yelled. My mother came in. "That's my little boy," she said. "Go away, I'll attend to him myself."

"Hurry, hurry," the man yelled. My mother came over and patted me on the head. I kept my eyes shut. "Wake up, angel, we have to take a trip. Remember? We told you we might have to go away again. And now it's happened. Be a good boy. Dress yourself, the way you always do."

"Hurry, hurry," the man yelled. Now the yelling came from a different room. I turned over and put the light out. I wanted to sleep. The light went on. "Hurry, hurry," I heard right near me. Somebody grabbed me by the arm and pulled off my covers. "Get moving." I screamed and pulled the blankets over my head with my free hand. My mother came in. She said to the man, "What's the matter with you? We have a right to put our clothes on, haven't we? Now you've made the child cry. I'd have gotten him up. Now it'll just take longer." "Hurry, hurry," the man yelled. "We've got to go, I have my orders." He slung his gun over his shoulder and left the room. The gun banged against the door. My mother said would I kindly dress myself the same as any other day because she had so many other things to do. She gave me a pair of trousers and told me to put them on. She wanted me to be ready when she came back. I began to dress, slowly. The man with the gun came to the door. "Hurry," he yelled again. I cried and threw a sock at him. He called my father. My father picked up the sock and said I shouldn't do such things. He helped me dress.

My mother came in and asked what I wanted to take with me on the trip. Then she ran out again. A little later the green man came to my door again. He held his gun to one side, but I had seen it. When he saw I was dressed, he left. "Hurry," he yelled again. "Hurry, hurry." My mother came and asked what I wanted to take, because the suitcases had to be closed. I couldn't think of anything. She grabbed my "sleepy blanket" and stuffed it in the suitcase. We put our coats on. Then I wanted to take my jumping jack. My mother said it was too late, because the suitcase was closed. I began to cry. My father said I'd have to carry the jumping jack myself. He took it down from the wall and gave it to me. They switched off the light and locked the door. We went down the stairs. My father was carrying two suitcases and my mother was carrying two carry-alls. I had to hold on to her coat. The soldier yelled, "Hurry" every time my father put the suitcases down for a second. We had a long way to go. I began to cry. My mother picked me up in her arms, but that didn't work. Then she took one of the suitcases and my father picked me up on his shoulders. The solider yelled, "Hurry." My mother said he should carry something if he was in such a hurry. He said he'd be glad to but it was forbidden. "Then we'll walk as slow as we please," said my mother. The soldier took her suitcase.

After we'd gone a long way, he put it down. He said, "Now you'll have to carry it yourself, or they'll see me." We turned a corner and then we had to go into a building.

There were lots of people in the building. We couldn't take two suitcases and two carryalls, they said. Only one suitcase for my father and one for my mother. My mother tried to take some things out of the carryalls and put them in the suitcases. She also took some things out of the suitcases and put them in the corner of the room.

The people said the soldiers were brutes. My mother said our soldier had carried a suitcase for us even though it was forbidden and they were only obeying orders. The other people were very down on the soldiers.

The door opened. Everybody stopped talking. Some more

people came into the room. Most of them had long black coats on.

A truck pulled up and we all had to get in. It was very crowded. All I could see was coats. When we got out we had to go into a big room full of people and tables. Lots and lots of people. There were people up in the balcony, too. I asked where we were. It was the theater, my father said. A place where they used to put on plays and people could go and see them. He showed me the stage and the curtain. We had to wait in line for a long time. Every so often we'd edge a little way forward along the tables. My father knew a lot of the people. They greeted him. They looked at him only for a second. He looked at the table. At every table they marked our papers with rubber stamps. It always took a long time. It was awfully crowded. I held my nose. More people kept coming in. My father lifted me up on his shoulders. Between the tables it was all full of heads. I said I saw Trude's head.

Then we had to go outside. All along the street there were people in black coats. We had to follow them. And behind us there were still more people. Here and there I saw a soldier with a gun. The people said we were going to Muiderpoort. At the end of the street my father said, "Look, there's Muiderpoort." It was a building with a gate you could pass through. What had become of all the people who had come down the street ahead of us? When we turned the corner, I saw them again, still walking. We weren't there yet. This was Muiderpoort, but we were going to Muiderpoort Station.

We got into the train. The people said we were going to Westerbork. I told them my mother and I had already been there. They asked my mother what it was like, and whether men and women stayed together. My mother said they slept separately but saw each other in the daytime. I asked if we'd be in our old shack again. My mother said she'd ask.

The train stopped a lot. Later we had to walk some more and stand in line again to get our papers stamped. My father asked if we'd been sent there by mistake. They made him show a lot more papers, but it wasn't a mistake. My father said we were hoping to immigrate to Palestine soon, we'd been waiting a long time. They asked for still more papers and said maybe we'd be able to immigrate soon.

By the number on the wood outside, I saw they hadn't given my mother and me the same shack as before.

My mother took the sheets out of the suitcase and made our bed. I went to bed with my jumping jack and my "sleepy." It was still light, but I was very tired. The people were talking and making a lot of noise.

WHITE DUNES

"This time it's different," my mother said. "This time there are three of us in the camp. This time we have everything we need—sheets and a book, for instance. This time it's not a mistake. We won't be going home tomorrow. We'll stay here or we'll go farther," she said. "But we'll have to wait again. Last time we had to wait for news that we were going home. This time we have to wait for news that we're going on, to Palestine."

My father told my mother that he had handed in all the papers and we had to wait for them to be stamped.

In the meantime my father taught me the Hebrew letters. I got them all mixed up, because he'd written them very close together on a little slip of paper. I couldn't see where one letter stopped and another started.

I also learned songs in a little class with other children. The other children knew most of the songs. They had been learning them much longer, the teacher said.

Then she couldn't come anymore. I didn't care, but from then on I had to take an afternoon nap.

One evening my mother said I didn't have to go to bed because we were going to meet some people in one of the shacks and sing songs. I asked if everybody would be there, and my father too. No, they wouldn't. That night it was the turn of the people in our shack. Other people went on other nights. I liked the idea. "But you'll have to promise," my mother said, "not to talk on the way and not to cry when we get there." I said

I wouldn't cry because I only cried in bed at night when my mother wasn't there. But now she'd be there too. We'd go together and stay together. I asked why I shouldn't ask any questions on the way, because my mother always told me to ask about everything. She said that what we were going to do wasn't really allowed, so we had to creep along quietly and then no one would notice. In that case, I said, I'd rather go to bed, but she said I'd be all alone in the shack because everybody was going, and there wouldn't be anybody to go and get her if I started crying. Then I started crying. She said I could do as I liked, but she was going to the singing. Besides, she said, it couldn't be so dangerous because everybody was going.

That night we crept through the darkness, keeping close to the brown wooden walls of the shacks. It was raining and cold. With one hand I clutched my mother's hand, and with the other I covered my mouth to make sure I wouldn't ask my mother something by mistake. The cold air made my nose hurt. My mother knocked on the door of the shack. It opened, and we went in quickly. Then it closed again. A whole lot of people were sitting there. They were little because they were sitting on low benches or on the floor. Most were wearing thick black coats. There was a lighted candle in one corner. My mother and I went and sat on a bench with other people. Everybody was wet. The air smelled wet. It wasn't as cold as outside, but it wasn't warm either.

A lot more people came in. We kept having to move over. I couldn't move my arms. All I could see was coats. I couldn't sit on my mother's lap because the people in front of us were much too close. But I was able to stand.

For a while there was whispering, then everybody was quiet. A lady stood up in the corner. She had a big bosom. She began to sing. More and more people joined in. They made a terrible racket. I looked at my mother, but she was singing too. I put my hands over my ears. People clapped.

The singer stopped and put her finger to her lips. The noise stopped. A woman came in, she was very angry. She asked if we were all out of our minds and told us to keep very quiet until the guard had passed. Then we could go on singing, but very softly, not so loud we could be heard in Amsterdam. Then she left. Someone blew the candle out. It was stuffy and dark. All those people breathing at once. I started breathing through my mouth because it made less noise. My mother put her arms around me and held me close. I could hear the steps outside more and more clearly. Someone was passing very slowly. Little by little the sound of the steps died away. I started breathing through my nose. Somebody sighed and then some other people sighed. The candle was lit again. The lady with the bosom stood up and said, "Softly now, very softly." Somebody asked if we shouldn't wait longer, but she said no, it had been the same on other evenings and we had someone watching outside.

She sang all kinds of songs and at the end she sang, "Where the white dunes." A lot of people joined in—softly. But they cried more than they sang. I asked my mother what dunes were, but she was crying too. I asked her why she was crying, and she said, "Because of the song." When it was over, the people slapped their coats, but not very loud. And they called out for the lady to sing it again.

And still another time. But then she sang only the last few lines. I was able to join in a little. My mother was crying so hard I almost had to cry too.

My mother helped me to undress. There was a lot of bustle in our shack because everybody was going to bed at once. My mother put me to bed and started undressing.

I woke up. I had to move over to make room for her. I asked her if she was sorry we had gone because the song had made her cry so. She said I was tired and she'd explain another time. She kissed me on the cheek and said good night.

ASSEMBLY

I woke up. I was scared. The siren was howling.

The last time the siren blew we had to crawl under our beds. There wasn't much room. A plane went rumbling overhead. My belly rumbled too. The rumbling seemed to come from the roof. It quieted down. We heard an explosion. We went out and looked. The people pointed at something, but I couldn't see what. My mother helped me. She told me to look where her fingers pointed. I saw a fire. She told me the plane had dropped a bomb on a farm. I saw yellow flames and black smoke. The people said the plane had crashed. I asked if a plane could crash on top of our shack. My mother said planes didn't drop bombs on shacks. After a while there was no more yellow fire, only black clouds of smoke.

I asked if I had to crawl under the bed. My mother gave me my clothes and told me to dress myself in a hurry. She herself was almost ready. When she was finished, she came and helped me. She didn't make me wash. People kept running out of our shack. It was already half empty. It was still dark. We met my father. People were coming from all directions, all going to the big field. There were lights overhead. If you looked carefully, you could see they were fastened to tall poles. We went and stood by the brown wooden wall of a shack. The light didn't shine on us. There were lots of people, in front of us and on both sides.

Where we were standing there was very little wind. I couldn't see anything but coats and snow. My father lifted me up on his shoulders. Under the light the white snow sparkled on black heads. Farther on, a man was standing in an open

space. It was cold. My father put me down on the ground. My
mother whispered that it wasn't so windy down there. I
crawled under my father's coat. It was warm there but very
dark. My legs and feet were freezing. I came out from under
my father's coat. I stamped my feet quietly to warm them.

Far away someone yelled, "Silence." Then a name was
called. The people looked around. Another name. Somebody
whispered, "Oh, him." Another name. Some people went past
us and left the field. I asked in a whisper if we could go too.
My father told me to listen carefully. If I heard our name, we
would leave too. I tried to understand the names, but it was
too hard. Numbers were called out too, and that made it even
harder. It went on a long time. "They're on the M's," my
mother said. "So pay close attention." My father and mother
held each other's hands. I couldn't understand a thing.

All of a sudden my father turned around. He kissed my
mother and she kissed him. They hugged each other. "Did you
hear that?" my mother asked me. "They've called our name."
I said I'd heard something like it, but I wasn't sure. My father
also said they'd called our name. They kissed me. "Now we're
going away. We're going to Palestine." I said I thought it was a
different name. When we left the field, the people shook hands
with us and patted my father on the back. They said, "Good
luck" and patted me on the head. My father and mother just
sighed. I asked my father why he didn't look at the people
when they spoke to us. I always had to look at anyone who
spoke to me. My mother said she'd explain later, now we had
to hurry. A lot of people went back to their shacks. Some were
crying.

In the shack my mother spread a sheet out on the bed. She
put all our belongings on it, because we weren't allowed to
take the suitcase. From time to time she tested whether the
sheet could still be knotted.

The bundle wouldn't hold anything like all our stuff. "We'll
just have to leave this book," my mother said. I didn't care, I
knew the book by heart. When we left the shack, our bed was
still covered with our things. "It won't make any difference,"

my father said, "once we're in Palestine." My father had his things tied up in a sheet too.

We crossed the crowded field. They weren't calling names anymore. The people looked at us. But we kept going.

We came to a freight car. The doors were open. People were climbing in. We had to wait in line.

Then we were in front. My father put his bundle into the car. The people inside shouted that it was full and no room for us. "But we're going too," my mother yelled. The people behind us ran to another car. It was full too. My father went to one of the cars and asked if there was still room for us three. My mother held my hand tight and looked inside too. "We've got a child with us," she called out. They let us in. First my mother's bundle went in, then my mother. Then my father put me in. It was dark. There was straw all over. The people were sitting or lying on it. They crowded together to make room for my mother and me. My mother put down her bundle and sat on it. There was room for me to sit on it too. My father was gone. I asked my mother where he was. She said he had gone to get his bundle. After a while he came back. He couldn't find it. He didn't remember exactly which car it was. The people in the car he thought said there wasn't any extra bundle. My mother said she'd seen the B. family in the car. My father wanted to go back. My mother said the train would be pulling out. It was getting light.

My father was gone a long time. Somebody closed one of the car doors. My mother got up and stumbled to the door. She leaned out and yelled my father's name. She yelled that the door had to be left open. She pointed and sang out, "There he comes." She pulled my father in and other people helped. They all fell in a heap. They shut the other door. It was dark. I asked if they were coming over to me. My mother said, "We'll come as soon as we get used to the darkness." Light came in through the cracks. Somebody tugged at the sliding doors, but he couldn't get them open. My mother sat back down on the bundle. My father came and stood with us. He hadn't found his bundle, but they said it would turn up later on. My mother took something out of our bundle. She said to me, "You've been awake almost the whole night. Now you have to sleep or you might get sick. I'm going to give you a pill to make you sleep." I said I could sleep without a pill. It wasn't a whole pill. It was only a little piece. There was nothing to drink. I collected spit and managed to get the pill down. It tasted nasty and crunched between my teeth. I stretched out because I couldn't sleep sitting up.

A whistle blew and I woke up. We went forward, backward, forward, backward. There was a jolt. My mother bumped her head against the wall. My father said we were pulling out and that's why it jolted so. The jolting got better. Somebody started singing. I knew the song. I joined in. *Ha-Tikvah*. I lay down again. My mother put her hand on my face. My father was sitting down too. I was tired. The engine was puffing far away. The car jiggled and rattled on the rails. The singing went on.

KITCHEN

In the new camp we never saw my father. As soon as we got there, he was sent to the other end. I couldn't remember much about getting there, because the pill had made me so sleepy.

My mother and I slept together in the top bunk, right under the slanting roof of the shack. The beds were much closer together and much narrower than in Westerbork. And here there were four-deckers. We had no sheets because my mother had given my father ours. She said, "Because he didn't find his bundle and he needs the sheets more than we do." My jumping jack had been lost and my "sleepy" was gone too. But a lady had some thread, and my mother hemmed a new three-cornered rag for me.

It was bad not being able to see my father because we were waiting to hear how he was getting ahead with our trip to Palestine. In the evening there was talk and people said nobody'd be going to Palestine. But somebody said, "Shh, there are children here." I pretended their talking didn't bother me. And after a while I really didn't hear it anymore.

I didn't eat much in that camp. My mother said I should eat more because I'd be sick if I didn't. But I wasn't hungry.

One day after lunch my mother took me to a place where the cooking pots were. They were big iron pots. There were lots of children. My mother said I had to help them carry the pots back to the kitchen. I asked if she'd come with me, but she said no, she couldn't. I'd just have to grab hold of a pot on one side and help carry it and run along with the others. Then we'd come back and she'd be waiting for me. I didn't feel like it at all because we had to go through the fence and across the road. There were soldiers all over with guns, and maybe they wouldn't let us come back. But my mother said I had to because all the children took turns helping and I hadn't done it yet, so now it was my turn. I started crying and said I really didn't want to. My mother patted me on the head and said I should do it to please her. If I didn't, they'd be angry with her because of my not wanting to help. I said I'd do it tomorrow, but that didn't work.

The handle was too high for me. The big children carried the pot. I just had to hold my hand on it. I said, in that case there was no point in my going along, but she said I should do it to show I meant well.

My mother waved at me and laughed. At the fence we had to wait awhile. Then the gate was opened. The soldiers picked up the lid of each pot and looked in. Our pot had no lid, so they let us right through. We had to walk a little way on the road. Then we came to the kitchen shack. It was blazing hot. A man was standing at the door with nothing on but long trousers. He showed us where to put the pots. He also said that we should clean out the pots right away and get them spic and span. There was a big noise, the children clattered the pot covers. The man asked if any more children were coming. Then he shut the door. He raised his hand and counted to three. Suddenly it was very still. All the children bent over the edges of the pots. Some couldn't keep their feet on the ground. All I could see was their backs and legs. Their heads and arms were gone. I'd have liked to help with the cleaning, but I didn't know how, and the man was in a big hurry. I went and stood beside our pot and tried to look over the edge. The children who had carried it were gone already. They were cleaning another pot. The man came over to me. He had a black moustache and beard. He looked into the pot and he looked at me. He saw that I hadn't cleaned the pot. He asked me if I could manage. I nodded, but he said I wouldn't be able to reach in. He turned a small pot upside down and put it beside the big one. "Stand up there," he said. I leaned over the edge of the big pot. The sides were full of yellow potato leavings.

After a while the man said we had to go back. When all the children were at the door, he asked, "Did it taste good?" They all shouted, "Yes." I'd had my head in the pot so long that I hadn't noticed anything good being handed out.

We went back to the fence. The soldiers pointed their fingers at us. The children said that was to count us. They counted about five times. Then they let us in. I waited until most of the children were gone. I looked for my mother, but she wasn't there. I started to cry. A big girl took me to my mother in our shack. My mother asked how it had been, and I told her. I told her I hoped the man wouldn't notice that I hadn't cleaned anything, but that I couldn't reach the inside. I said he hadn't given me anything to clean the pot with, and the other children had gotten something good to eat from him, but not me. So he must have noticed that I hadn't cleaned the pot.

My mother screamed at me, "You didn't clean the pot? You didn't eat anything?" I said the man didn't tell us to eat the pot clean, he only told us to clean it. And she hadn't told me either. She was very angry. First at me, then at the man. She took me around to see a lot of people. I kept having to tell the whole story, and she pretended to be very angry. A lady said I'd have to wait a week and then I could go and help carry the pots again. She asked me if I'd enjoyed it, and I said yes I had.

Every day after lunch, a little while after the pots had been taken away, I could hear a loud "yes" from the kitchen shack on the other side. I stood by the fence with the other children and listened. I'd heard that sound before, but I'd never known what it was.

The next week I had another chance to go. When I came in, the man looked at me. "I'll be right over to help you," he said. "You've been here before, haven't you?" When the door was closed, he came over to me. He picked me up and started putting me into the big pot. I asked if he'd take me out again. "Of course I will," he said. There were no other children on that pot. "Now make it quick, start eating," he said. I asked him what with. He collected a bit of food in his fingers and put it in his mouth. I told him my mother didn't let me lick my fingers. "I let you," he said. I didn't know what to do. The other children were licking their fingers. I was just going to start cleaning out the pot with my fingers when the man came and gave me a shiny silver spoon.

The pot wasn't completely empty when the man called out that we had to go. I went on eating, but he lifted me out and put me down on the ground. He let me keep the spoon, but he told me to hide it carefully under my clothes.

This time I found my way back to our shack alone. My mother was very happy. I told her the man in the kitchen was a good kraut like the one in Amsterdam who'd helped her with the suitcase. She laughed and said he wasn't a kraut at all, he was Mr. L., whom I knew—Marion's father, remember, Mrs. L.'s daughter? I knew Mrs. L. and I knew Marion all right. But I couldn't believe that this was Mr. L. He didn't look at all like him.

CAKE

My mother woke me up. She put her fingers to her lips. There wasn't a sound in the shack. She whispered. She told me to dress quickly. She said she had a surprise for me. I had to put on my coat and my mittens. We went out on tiptoes. It was getting light. We stopped for a moment outside the door. All I could hear was the wind in the trees on the other side of the road. I couldn't see the trees. My mother looked around. She took my hand. I wanted to ask her something, but she said psst. She pulled me gently along. It was cold.

My mother had a package under her arm. She didn't tell me what it was. And she didn't tell me what we were going to do. She walked very fast.

We came to the door of a shack and knocked softly. Someone inside said something and my mother whispered something at the door. The door opened and we stepped into the darkness. We hadn't met anybody on the way. My mother put the package down on a bench. The man who had let us in said something I didn't understand and held out his hand. I went and stood right beside my mother. She gave him something and he held it up to his eyes. "That wasn't our agreement," he said. "You'll get the rest afterward," my mother said, "when it's all over." "Nothing doing," said the man. "Everything right away or the deal is off. Our agreement was all at once. I'm not taking any chances." "But what if it doesn't go through?" "You won't be the first. Don't you trust me?"

My mother gave him something else. He opened a door and let us in. There was a little more light. We kept our coats on because it was cold. There was a brown wooden table and a green wooden bench on the brown wooden floor. There was a window on each side, high up on the walls. My mother put the package down and told me I could sit down. She walked back and forth. There was another door across from the one we had come in by. She listened at that door and walked around again. "It's taking so long," she said. She went to our door, opened it and called the man. He came and said we should keep still. Everything would be all right, but we had to be patient. He said we'd come much too early and that was dangerous enough. He said my mother should sit down and stop roaming around and not call him again. She should count slowly to a thousand and then she could call again if necessary. He shut the door. My mother went back to the door and listened. I counted slowly to a thousand, but I got mixed up.

All of a sudden the other door opened. My mother stood still. Somebody came in. He stopped by the door. I was pretty sure I knew him, but he was standing in the dark. I went over to my mother. She was standing by the table, looking at him. He looked at her. I saw she was scared. I grabbed hold of her coat. "Be still," he said. "Don't say anything. I don't want to know." I knew the voice too. He came over to us. They hugged each other. I stood behind her back. My mother cried.

Then she wiped her tears away. She said to me, "Don't you know your daddy?" He said to me, "I know I've changed, with my beard and my bald head. Do you still know me?" He took hold of me gently. I knew it was my father by the feel of his hand. I let him pull me. He hugged me. But there was a lot of coat and hair between us.

My mother said we'd brought a package for my father and she gave it to him. She told me we should sing because it was his birthday. I said the man had told us not to make noise. I congratulated my father and repeated the words my mother had told me. "No poem this time," said my father, "but next time I'm counting on a big long song." And he hugged me.

Then he opened the package. A real round cake came out. He asked how my mother had made it. She took a spoon out of her coat. I said the man in the kitchen had given it to me, but of course my father could use it. He took a spoonful. I saw it wasn't a real cake after all. It was potatoes and pieces of bread pressed together. In the last few days my mother hadn't made me clean my plate, she'd been very nice and only asked me if I'd had enough. And then quickly she'd whisked my plate away.

"You shouldn't have done that," my father said. "You must have starved yourself for a week to make this cake." "It's from both of us," my mother said. "You need it more than we do." My father began to eat. He asked if I wanted some too, but I wasn't hungry.

He asked if I took good care of my mother. I couldn't think of an answer. My mother said I took good care of her, but that I cried a lot and didn't eat much. My father said I should eat properly because I'd get sick if I didn't, and he didn't want that.

I asked him if I could sit on his shoulders the way I used to. He said yes I could and he stood up. But he couldn't lift me. My mother said I was much too heavy for him. He said, "Don't worry. We'll manage." He helped me to climb on the bench. And for once they let me stand on the table in my shoes. He sat down and I climbed up on his shoulders. He let me ride picka-back, and he walked around with me. My mother helped me down. My father had to eat some more because there wasn't much time.

We watched him eat. When he had finished, they looked at each other. My father said it must be time. My mother said the man would let us know five minutes ahead. They walked around the room together, talking. My mother whispered something and hugged my father. He said, "Oh no, we can't do that." "Why not?" said my mother. "I know how much you want to, it'll be all right." "But what about the child?" my father asked. "He won't notice," my mother said. But he said it wouldn't do. "Then he'll just have to wait outside," my mother said. And she came over to me and told me to say good-bye to my father, and then to wait in the corridor until she came out. I didn't want to. My father said, "Let him stay. We don't really have to." My mother said to me, "You do as you're told," and took me out of the room. She asked the man if I could stay there awhile and then she went back inside. I sat down on the floor in the dark, right beside the door. I could hardly see him in the dark.

I heard my father and mother in the room. I asked the man if I could have a little water to drink, but he said no. I couldn't understand what my father and mother were saying. But it sounded as if they were quarreling. My father's groans and my mother's screams got louder and louder. I stood up and started to go in. "Not there," the man said. "Go sit down." I started to cry. The man said, "Be still. Your mother will be out in a minute." He gave me some water, but I kept on crying. He pulled me away from the door. "If you don't stop, I'll put you outside, hear?" I screamed, "No. Don't do that." He got mad and knocked on the door. My mother yelled that it couldn't be time yet. He yelled back that they'd have to let me in because my screaming would give everything away. My mother came out and told me to keep quiet. My father yelled that she should bring me in with her. "You can stay with us, but then you must sit over there and keep your eye on the door and tell us if somebody knocks." I said I would. She went over to my father. They whispered. Then I heard my mother breathing hard. My head turned in their direction. My father looked over my mother's shoulder. He had his arms around her. They were moving up and down. My father said to me, "Keep your eye on the door." But my head stayed turned.

"It's no good," my father said. "Anyway, it's almost time. It's no good in such a hurry."

The man knocked and called out, "Five minutes more." My mother turned around and pulled her coat tight. She came over to me and took me by the hand. She pulled me through the door and told the man to let me out and not let me back in, even if I cried. She said to me, "I won't be long. Wait outside and don't cry or I never want to see you again." She left me there and went into the room. The man looked out through a little hole, opened the door and pushed me out. I sat down on the wooden steps and waited.

My mother came out a little later. She walked fast, I had to run to keep up with her and she wouldn't wait. There were lots of people.

———

The next day was my birthday. I asked if there was a cake for me too. My mother said she'd used everything up for my father. This time I wouldn't get anything, but the next time I'd get whatever I wanted. I wanted a new jumping jack and a dump truck and to steer the ferry myself.

NOSE THUMBING

I'd helped to carry the cooking pots and we were back in the camp. I didn't go straight to my mother, I stayed with some children who were hanging around. We walked slowly along the barbed wire on our way back to the shacks. The sun was shining and I was hot. Some big children ahead of me were whispering. All of a sudden they stopped. I asked them what was wrong. They said that I shouldn't look but a big palooka was coming our way. I looked and saw a soldier in a green uniform with a big brown dog. The dog look like the wolf in *Little Red Riding Hood*, but the kraut was holding him on a chain. The children said I mustn't look, and they all stood with their backs to the road so I couldn't see. A big girl asked me, "Have you got a tongue?" A few of the children ran away. I nodded. She said, "Then let's see it. I don't believe you." I looked at the others. A boy came over and grabbed hold of me. "All right, let's see it." I opened my mouth and stuck my tongue out. Some more children ran away. A big boy who was standing in front of me took a step to one side. I shut my mouth again. Some kids shouted b-aa-aah. A girl said to me, "I bet you wouldn't dare stick your tongue out at a kraut." I looked at her and stuck my tongue out. "No," she said. "Not at us. Do it so he can see it. And thumb your nose." I said I didn't know what that meant, and some of the children laughed. The boy who was right in front of me spread his fingers and put the thumb of one hand on his nose and the thumb of the other hand on the little finger of the first hand. I knew all about that but just didn't know what it was called. The girl asked if I'd do it to the kraut. I nodded. The children ran away.

I went over to the fence. The rusty brown barbed wire was strung so close together that I could hardly see through. My hand certainly wouldn't have gone through. I took a step back. On the other side of the fence there were green weeds. Then came the gray path. Over there the kraut with the dog was walking back and forth. I spread my fingers, put my thumb on my little finger and stuck both hands on my nose. It was hard holding them straight. Then I stuck my tongue out and shouted booh the way children were always doing. Somebody grabbed my arm and pulled me away. It was a girl. She said I was crazy and I should stop this minute. The other children stood nearby, looking on. The girl took my hands off my nose and turned me around. I turned back and stuck my tongue out as far as I could. She gave me a slap and pulled me away from the fence. The children ran away when we came near them. I let her pull me and stuck my tongue out at everybody we passed. With my free hand I half-thumbed my nose. After a while we came to our shack. The girl dragged me inside and took me to my mother. She told her what I had done. My mother said, "What!" and slapped my face hard. My ears rang and my cheek smarted, but I didn't cry. I told her about the kraut and the police. I said the children were afraid to stick their tongues out and they thought I'd be afraid too. And I told her this girl had been there when the children told me what to do. And how they promised that if I did it the big children would let me play with them.

My mother asked the girl if it was true and she said yes, it was. Then my mother said the girl would hear a thing or two from her own mother, but that she was mighty glad all the same that she'd made me stop and brought me back to her.

The girl went away. My mother began to cry. She said, "Do you realize what you've done? Do you want them to kill us all? Why do you do such things? Do you promise never to do it again?" I said I didn't know yet because the kraut hadn't seen anything because he had already passed when I did it and he hadn't turned around. My mother screamed that I was out of my mind and how lucky I'd been that the soldier hadn't turned around because he'd have sicked the dog on me and had her shot. And that could still happen because another soldier could have seen it.

I said there hadn't been any other krauts around. "What about the guards?" she said. I didn't know what she was talking about. She stood up and pulled me outside with her. There was a whole crowd of mothers.

"Now listen carefully," my mother said. "I'm going to show you something without using my finger. And you mustn't point either. And you mustn't look that way too long. Just do exactly as I say. Look over my shoulder. Do you see the watchtower?"

All I could see was the shacks and behind them some tall poles. I told her so. "And what do you see on top of those poles?" she asked. I looked a little higher and I saw some kind of a hut. I told her so.

"That hut is the watchtower. There's a watchtower on every side of the camp. Didn't you know that?" I said I hadn't known and besides the poles were outside the barbed wire so they didn't belong to our camp. My mother said, "All right, now turn around when I do and you'll see another watchtower. And inside it you'll see a soldier. He's on guard and he sees everything. But you mustn't look at him too long. Just keep turning and don't stop." I did what she said and I saw another watchtower with a soldier walking around inside. "Did you see him?" my mother asked. I nodded. "He sees you wherever you are. And if he doesn't see you, another guard is sure to see you. Let's hope they didn't see you sticking your tongue out."

My mother left me standing and went over to the other mothers. There were lots of children around our shack too. The mothers were arguing about which children should get the worst punishment. It was about me too. But my mother said I had done it because the big children had put me up to it. I stood looking at the first watchtower. All of a sudden I saw a soldier in it. He was holding a gun that was pointed over one side. He moved around slowly and turned in my direction. His gun moved with him until it was aimed straight at me. And there he stopped. He looked at me. I heard a bang. The women

and children screamed. My mother came over to me, grabbed
my hand and pulled me into the shack. I began to cry.

My mother comforted me. She said he had fired only because
too many people were standing in one place and that was forbidden. She said they didn't shoot at people right away, they
fired warning shots in the air.

Next day I ran into the other children. But they didn't let me
stay with them. "Because," they said, "you told your mother
we put you up to it." I said I hadn't told her anything. But the
girl they could have asked wasn't there. They said she was sick
or something.

SHADE

Almost everybody was asleep in our shack, but my mother was on duty. That's why we were dressed so early. Trude came in. She said my father was back at the infirmary and that my mother should bring his clean linen and take his clothes away. Trude didn't have much time, so she didn't stay long. My mother was upset because she couldn't go to my father on account of her duty. She gave me the things and told me to run right over and tell my father she'd come as soon as her work was done.

I knew the way because my father had been in the infirmary a week before. We'd gone to see him every day. The first day I hadn't recognized him because they'd shaved his beard. And his eyes were very big when he was awake. But he'd slept a lot in the infirmary. My mother had said that he wasn't really well when they let him out. "It won't last," she said. I was sorry because we couldn't see each other anymore. It's true, he'd been sick, but at least we'd been able to see each other every day. He had smiled when he left. He hadn't minded very much. "The doctor can't help it," he'd said. "He can't let me lie around here forever."

I couldn't see why my mother had been so upset. She herself had expected it the whole time. I was glad I'd be seeing him again.

I knocked at the door of the infirmary. Somebody opened and I said I'd come to see my father and my mother was coming later when she'd finished with her duty. "What's your name?" I said my name. "Go straight to your mother and tell her to come here immediately, or it will be too late." I asked if he was better. "He won't be here long, tell your mother to come quick." I said in that case I didn't need to take his clothes. But they put his shoes into my hand and sent me away.

Outside the infirmary there was a grass plot. The sleeping shacks began a little farther on. It was already light and the sun was shining on the green grass. I walked on the grass. It was wet and the drops of water sparkled. I stopped walking and kicked at the grass. The big drops fell but the grass was still wet. I put my hands in my father's shoes and walked on four shoes in the grass. Close up like that the raindrops sparkled even more. The light in the drops didn't stand still, it moved. I couldn't blow the drops off the blades of grass.

When I got to the end of the grass plot and came to the brown sand path by the sleeping shacks, I stood up on my two feet. But I kept my father's shoes on my hands. The sun was shining on the brown wall of one shack, it reached up pretty near to the edge of the roof. The path and the wall of the next shack were dark, almost black. I hugged the black wall so as to keep out of the sun. When I got to the end of the shack, I had to make myself very thin and walk sideways along the wall under the overhanging roof. Otherwise, I'd have been in the sun. I slipped along the side and then along the end, and then I had to cross over to the next shack. I went down on my hands and knees and crawled under the sun. Then I was in the shade on the side of the next shack.

All of a sudden I was back at the infirmary. I went back the same way to the place where I'd crossed over. I stuck to the shady ends and kept crawling in the shade to the next shack. At the end of the path I came to the shade of a long shack. And there I kept going. So I stayed in the shade of the shacks.

After a while I came to another crossing, but this time I couldn't keep out of the sun, because the sun was shining on the path. It was broad daylight. I jumped through the sunny patch. It shined in my eyes. I heard a scream and I looked around.

I didn't know those shacks at all, and the numbers were all wrong. Someone came along and I asked for our shack. She showed me the way, but I had to ask five other people before I found our shack. I went in. My mother was back from her work. She was making our bed. She asked me if I'd given her message right. I nodded and gave her the shoes. She looked at them and put them under the bed. I went outside and joined the children who were hanging around near the door. When I got there they stopped talking for a second, but then they started up again.

Trude came along. She asked where my mother was, and I said she was in the shack. She ran in. A little later she came out again and asked me if I'd told my mother to go straight to the infirmary. I said I'd forgotten. My mother came out and asked why I hadn't given her the message. I said she'd been on duty and I'd been lost and besides I'd forgotten. She said she was going out and I should wait in the shack for her and she couldn't say when she'd be back. I said I wanted to go with her, but she said I couldn't. She said my father might die, and that wasn't anything for babies. I said I wasn't a baby, and he was my own father and I had a perfect right to be there when he died, and all the children I knew had been there when their fathers died. My mother asked, "Who, for instance?" I pointed at one of the boys, but she said his father was still alive. Luckily another boy said he'd been allowed to be there and a girl said so too. They were brother and sister, but I didn't tell my mother that. Then my mother said, "All right, but only until it happens. Then you'll have to leave." I promised I would. We ran to the infirmary together. I ran ahead and showed her the shortest way, but she wanted to take the way she knew for fear of getting lost.

The doctor opened the door to the infirmary. He said, "At last. You're lucky you're not too late." I told my mother she could see for herself that my father was still there. The doctor pointed to a bed farther down, and he himself went the other way. My mother went to my father's bed. He was sleeping. She put her hand on his forehead and whispered his name in his ear. But he went on sleeping. The doctor came over. My mother was crying. "If only I had come sooner," she said, "I could have talked to him." The doctor asked her why she was so late, and she said I hadn't told her. The doctor said that Trude had gone to tell her early that morning, but it wouldn't have made any difference because my father was so far gone he had slept the whole time and he couldn't have said anything. But the doctor said anyway he was glad my mother had come in time. He nodded his head in my direction and asked my mother, "Does he

know . . . ?" My mother said I knew my father might die, and I
wanted to be there because he was my father and because I'd
heard from other children that they'd been allowed to stay
there while their father was dying. I said it wasn't true and I
had just wanted to be with my father and my mother because
my father had told me to take good care of her.

We stood by my father's bed. After a while my mother went
outside for a minute. When she was gone, my father sighed. I
ran out to get her, but when we came back, he was sleeping
quietly again.

My mother felt his pulse and counted. My father turned
over on his side. My mother whispered his name and told him
we were there with him. I said he couldn't hear anything, but
she said yes he could.

The doctor came by and my mother went up to him. They
stood talking at the foot of the bed. My mother wanted him to
give my father an injection that would make him well. But he
said it wouldn't help and he didn't have any injections. My
mother said she knew he still had some and she'd give anything if only he'd give my father an injection. The doctor said
one injection wouldn't do my father any good, it would take a
whole lot of injections, and he didn't have enough. Besides, he
said, in a few days my father would have to leave the infirmary
and go to work. And then he'd be back again in a day or two.
If he even made it back. Now at least he was sleeping peacefully, and he'd pass on peacefully in his sleep without noticing.
He had so few injections, and he had to save those few for his
patients who didn't sleep so peacefully, who were in pain, and
were far from dead. So they talked and they talked.

I stood beside my father's bed. His head stuck out from
under the covers. He was lying on his side with his face toward
me. The beard on his cheeks and chin had grown a little. Our
faces were right near each other. I held my head at a slant so as
to look him straight in the face. It was really my father. I recognized his closed eyelids, his nose, his mouth and his ears.
His cheeks were thin, but they were still like my father's
cheeks, the way I'd known them early in the morning in bed;
my father who had held me on his lap; who had let me ride

horseback on his knee. But I was afraid to get too close to his face, because he was sick. I listened to see if I could hear him breathe. He breathed so softly and my mother and the doctor were making so much noise that I couldn't hear a thing. But I think I saw the blanket move a little.

Suddenly he turned over on his back. He swallowed. He heaved a deep sigh and opened his eyes. He looked surprised, but the doctor had told us that he'd been asleep when they brought him in. So he probably didn't know where he was. He opened his mouth wide to say something. But then a funny thing happened: He couldn't get it closed again. He wanted to say something, but he couldn't. You could hear his breath, but not a word came out.

I turned around and went to the foot of the bed. The doctor was standing with his back to me. I heard my mother's voice from the other side, but I couldn't see her. I pushed him aside and tugged at my mother's clothes because she wouldn't listen to me. I screamed that my father wanted to say something, but he couldn't because he couldn't get his mouth closed, and she should help him.

The doctor turned around and said, "It's all over." My mother cried and went to my father. She put her hands on his cheeks and kissed him on the forehead. I said that was dangerous, but she said I had to go away because it was all over and I had promised to go away when that happened. The doctor came up and passed his hand over my father's face. I asked why he did that and my mother said it was to close his eyes. I looked at my father's eyes. They were closed now. "Now go outside, the way you promised." I nodded and started away from the head of the bed.

In turning over, my father had pushed the white sheet aside and put his hand down beside it. My mother and the doctor were standing by his head. I went slowly up to the bed and lifted my hand. My hand glided over the white sheet and the sleeve of my father's pajama coat and came to his hand. It was cold. I let my hand slide over his. The doctor and my mother had their backs turned to me. Quickly I gave his hand a kiss, and then I ran out of the infirmary. Outside, I wiped my lips on my sleeve. Then I sat down on the steps outside the door and waited.

I waited a long time. I was cold. Trude came and asked why I was sitting out in the cold. I told her they'd let me be there when my father died, but I'd had to promise to go away after that, and that was why I was sitting outside. She took me in with her and told my mother that she'd found me out in the cold and I could get very sick. She asked my mother if she'd gone crazy. My mother said I should have gone back to our shack. I said she hadn't told me to.

My father was lying under a sheet. I wanted to show him to Trude, but they wouldn't let me. After that I had to wait a long time on the other side of the infirmary, and they wouldn't let me see what they were doing.

We went back to our shack. It was dark and most of the people in the shack were already sleeping. Some people whispered something to my mother and she whispered something back. In bed I began to cry. My mother asked if I was crying because my father was dead. I said yes I was but also because I was afraid of dying myself. She said that I really wasn't going to die and that Trude had frightened me with her talk about getting sick. I said that wasn't it, but because I'd kissed my father's hand and I'd die on account of that and my mother would die because she'd kissed his forehead, which was even worse. My mother hugged me and kissed me and said I certainly wouldn't die from kissing my father's hand, and I wouldn't get sick either and neither would she. I said she had told me herself not to kiss anyone in the camp because it was dangerous. She kissed me again and said, "We often kiss each other. That's not so bad, because we're the same family. But you must never kiss a stranger or let a stranger kiss you. And especially you must never kiss anyone on the lips, because that's really dangerous. But I'm sure we won't get sick from kissing Daddy's hand or his forehead."

I was very tired. I crawled under the covers and my mother stayed with me.

DREADHOUSE

The next day the big children let me go with them because my father had died and I had been there. I wasn't a baby anymore. But I had to promise not to snitch, and they said there'd be some other test for me to go through. They didn't know yet what. We went across the field. We met the little children and they asked me if I wanted to play with them. But I said I was in a hurry and besides I wasn't a baby anymore, and didn't they know my father was dead?

We kept on going. There was a big boy on each side of me. And more ahead of us, and a few girls too. I was the littlest, but that was because my mother was kind of short and my father wasn't very big either. We were coming close to the dreadhouse. One of the big boys asked me if I'd dare to go in. He said it was forbidden and besides it was dangerous. I asked why, but he couldn't say. Another boy said I had promised to go through a test and this was it. I should go into the house and stay there until they called me to come out. I said I was willing, but I didn't know what was in this dreadhouse. I asked if they'd all been inside, and they said, "Naturally." I said I'd go in if somebody went with me. And if it wasn't too scary, I'd stay there alone until they called me. At first nobody wanted to go with me. But I said if they'd all been there, they had nothing to be afraid of. Then a few of the children whispered something to each other.

I was getting cold because we'd been standing still for ages. My feet had been cold a long time from the snow and now my body was getting colder and colder. I stretched out my arms and slapped my sides, and I stamped my feet at the same time.

One of the big boys did the same. Then he said, "All right, I'll go in with you."

The other children went a few steps away. The boy pressed the door handle gingerly. It was a gray iron door and hard to open. Inside it was dark. The boy held his nose with his thumb and forefinger and beckoned to me. There was a high doorstep. I stepped over it. Inside there was nothing to be seen, everything was black. The boy opened the door part way and went ahead, grazing the wall with one hand. He opened a wooden door and told me to come along. He sounded funny because of holding his nose. I didn't see much. There were white things lying on the floor and in a pile next to the dark wall. There was another pile in the middle with something sticking out on all sides.

Some other children came in. Most were holding their noses. A girl said to me, "Look, there's your father. He hasn't even got a sheet."

Then I saw the dead people. There were bundles of bodies. Some of the bundles had arms and legs sticking out. There were naked human bodies. Some still had trousers on. They were all mixed up, thrown in helter-skelter. One was lying on his back at the top of a pile with his head hanging down. I looked at his face. He had big dark eyes. His arms were dangling. He was very thin. Another was lying with one arm sticking out and his head on top of it. The other arm was missing. There were also separate arms and legs. Behind me I heard something click. I looked around and saw that the children had gone away or else they were hiding in the dark. The outside door was shut. I turned back to the bodies. I tried to find my father. I twisted my head in all directions, to the side, upside down, so as to look straight at the faces which were tilted every which way. But they all looked so terribly alike. And there was so little light. Straight in front of me there was a bundled sheet at the top of a pile. I could see there was a body in it. Could that be my father? A naked corpse was lying face down in front of me. The head was turned to one side. They were all bald. My father wasn't there. He was probably still in the infirmary. After a while they'd bury him. I took another good look at the bodies. They were gray. The dirty sheets looked white beside them. I went back and shut the wooden inside door. I went to the outside door. There was no handle to open it with. I banged, but it didn't do any good. I heard the children outside.

I went to the other door and opened it again. I went in and stepped over the first bodies. I climbed up on the pile and looked into the topmost bundled sheet. All I could see was an arm. I started to unwrap the sheet. I heard them yelling outside. I pulled out the arm. The hand was like my father's. I tugged at the sheet until I could see the face. The face was black with beard. I climbed down off the pile and saw a body to one side. It wasn't getting much light. I looked at the face. The eyes were black. The cheeks were thin. The beard was short like my father's. The nose was like his, too. I looked at the hands. They were like my father's. But the body wasn't at all like my father's.

Somebody grabbed hold of me and pulled me away. "Are you crazy? Do you want to die? It's very dangerous. Come on. We've been shouting at you for hours to come out." I said I was looking for my father and I couldn't get the door open. "Your father isn't here," the boy said. He pulled me out, slammed the door and told me to run away.

Pretty soon we caught up with the other children. One of the girls said, "Your father hasn't even got a sheet." I said he was in a sheet and I'd seen it myself. She said she saw him too, and it wasn't true. The boy who had pulled me out said my father wasn't there at all, but when the others went booh and said they bet he was scared he said he'd only said that because I was so little. I said I was big and I knew perfectly well my father was in there and I'd seen him in a sheet and I could show him to anybody who wanted to see. But nobody wanted.

The girl said, "Seeing you know everything, tell us what they do with the bodies." I said I knew all right, but I wouldn't tell them, because I'd done what I was supposed to, and the test was all over. If she wanted to know, I'd tell her if she went in with me. But she didn't want to and the children yelled booh at her. Then we went somewhere else and the big children let me stay with them.

In the evening my mother asked what I'd done that day. I told her I'd gone with the big children. She asked how I'd managed that, and I said they'd let me because I'd gone through a test. I'd been in the dreadhouse. She asked what the dreadhouse was. I said she must know, it was the place where they put the bodies, and she must know, too, that they'd chucked my father in there, and she must know, too, that he didn't even have a sheet. I told the other children he had one, though I'd seen him myself without a sheet. And I screamed that she must be crazy to let them chuck him in there without a sheet, and she hadn't even told me they'd taken him out of the infirmary because then I could have gone and said good-bye to him, and I thought it was disgusting and it was her fault if he was in there all naked with the bodies. My mother only said, "No" and "It's not true," but I didn't listen and I said there was no point in lying to me because I'd seen it with my own eyes. And I started crying something terrible.

My mother said it wasn't a dreadhouse but a deadhouse. But that was all one to me. She also said that the dead people's bodies were taken there because they needed the beds in the infirmary for other sick people. And that men came every day and took the bodies away and buried them out in the woods. But it so happened that they hadn't come today. And she also said my father was in a sheet, but I hadn't seen him because all the sheets looked the same, and also because so many people had died after him and they were on top of the pile, and he was way down below.

My mother hugged me and stroked me and kissed me. Then she started crying, too, and said it was no fun for her either.

Later she asked me who had told me to go looking in the deadhouse. I told her one of the big boys had pulled me out and had told me it was dangerous. My mother asked if I'd touched anything, and I told her I'd looked for my father. She took me with her. She poured some disinfectant in a basin of water and washed me all over. It stank. She said I should never do it again. She asked me who sent me to the deadhouse. I said I wasn't a baby anymore and I had promised not to snitch, and I wouldn't tell her. Then my mother asked who the boy was who had taken me away. All I knew was that his name was Jaap. She took me out with her. She found out from Jaap who the others were. My mother told some of the other mothers what had happened. They asked if she had given me a good disinfecting. Then they went and disinfected their own children. They were all furious because the door of the deadhouse could be opened so easily. They said it was disgraceful and a lock should be put on it right away.

The next day all the children stank of disinfectant. One of the children suggested going back to the dreadhouse. I told him it was a deadhouse, not a dreadhouse, and they'd locked it and besides all the bodies had been taken away.

We went. The handle was gone from the door.

SOUP

My mother woke me up. It was dark. If we wanted to go to Palestine with the others, we'd have to be out by the fence in two minutes, ready to get into the train. People were running out of the shack. I had to put my shoes on and button my coat over my pajamas. My mother put our clothes in a pile with the things she always kept ready in a cloth. She tied the cloth half-way and pulled the knot tight on the way. There were still people in the shack when we left, but it was so dark I couldn't see how many.

The gate through the fence was open and we saw people running out ahead of us. We ran after them. It was cold.

The train was full and dark. The people helped us get in. In this train there were benches to sit on.

I asked my mother why this train didn't jolt so when we started moving. She said she didn't know and I should sleep.

I woke up and heard people talking, but it was still quiet. It was light. I opened my eyes and I saw cloud shapes through the window. They were white against the blue sky. I sat up. The grass outside was standing still. I told my mother the train had stopped. She said, "Oh, so you've finally woken up?" She told me the train had been standing still for more than a day. "Didn't you notice?" she asked me. I shook my head and looked at the people next to me and across from us on the benches. A few people were sleeping sitting up. My mother said, "Say thank you to Mrs. P., the lady beside you. She's been kind enough to keep your feet on her lap."

I looked at the woman beside me. I said, "Thank you" very

quietly. She said, "My, how you've slept. Your mother's arm is all stiff. Now at least we can stand up for a while." I was sitting on my mother's lap. I moved away from Mrs. P. a little to let her stand up. But she didn't move. My mother asked if she could stand up for a little while. She put me down on the floor but held on to me. When she stood up, she let me sit down in her place. She squeezed past the legs in the center aisle. There she stood still. From time to time she took a few steps or moved her arms up and down, first one, then the other. I asked if she was cold. She said, "My legs are a little cold, but mostly they're stiff from sitting so long." I looked out at the grass, the clouds and the sky. Then I looked at my mother again. I asked her if it would be much longer before the train got to Palestine. The people on the opposite bench looked at me and then they looked at my mother. She said, "I don't know. We don't know where we are." I was just going to ask if my father didn't know either, but suddenly I remembered that he was dead. I changed my sentence so she wouldn't notice I'd forgotten, and asked why the train had stopped.

My mother said she didn't know either. A lady said we might have to go back. I asked if we were already far from Bergen-Belsen. She said, "A long way, I think, but we can't be sure, because the train kept going in different directions, first to the east for a whole day and then it stopped for hours, and then a whole day to the north."

I looked at her and said that we'd only gotten into the train the night before. My mother came over to me. She made me stand up and took me on her lap again. She made me sit with my face turned toward her. She put her arms around me and held me tight. I looked at her mouth. "Don't you know we've been sitting in this train for almost two weeks? Don't you know the train kept stopping and then starting up again, forward or backward? Don't you remember that you woke up now and then? You even made peepee in the pottie, remember? And you said you were so hungry. You must remember that. And how I helped you take your coat off because it was so hot in the train because we'd been standing in the sun all day? And later you were cold again, remember, and you wanted to put your coat back on over your pajamas. Don't you remember?" I heard her talking and I could see she'd be miserable if I didn't know. I stroked her cheek and said she'd probably dreamed it all, but that didn't matter, because we were together in the train again.

The lady who'd let me put my feet on her lap sat up a little straighter and began to say something. My mother let me go and touched her for a second and she stopped talking and leaned back again. My mother hugged me tighter and stroked my hair. "Your hair is growing nicely again," she said. "The clipping did you good, the lice are all gone." And she told me again all the things she had dreamed. And she kept saying that I must know. I saw how the whole business upset her.

She had already told me most of the things several times. But then she said, "You must remember how I wanted to leave you alone when I had to go to the toilet, but you wouldn't let me go and you cried?" She hadn't said that before. So I said yes, I'd suddenly remembered. "And that you were hungry?" I said very slowly that I was beginning to remember that too, but that I'd slept so hard I wasn't sure. My mother said she could understand that. "You see you remember," she said, and she hugged me.

Then she let me get up and go into the center aisle. I couldn't move around much in the aisle because people were sitting and lying all over.

I looked through the window on the other side. We were right near the trees. Someone was climbing slowly between the trees, up the slope away from the train. I pointed my finger at him and turned around to my mother. My mother was looking at the man, too. The people said, "He's running away"; "We can get out"; "The man has gone crazy"; "They'll shoot him dead."

More people climbed up the slope, I heard doors slamming and people shouting outside. Somebody shouted, "The door's open." The people had stood up and I couldn't see anything. My mother called me. I heard her coming closer. Somebody pushed me toward her and she grabbed me by the arm and pulled me over to our place. She sat down again and I was beside her on the bench. A few other people were still sitting, but most had gotten out. I asked if we could get out too. My mother said no, we couldn't. I said I wanted to very badly and everybody else was getting out. My mother just sat there with her eyes closed. She leaned her head against the wall. Then she slowly got up and told me to stay there till she came back. She went to the door and I heard her talking with the people outside. A little later she came back. She said I could get out with Trude, but I should do exactly what Trude said. I promised I would and Trude helped me down off the footboard. She took hold of me and I had to jump from the lowest step to the road-bed. My mother went back inside. We climbed a little way into the woods. I waved at my mother in the train. There were still a few people behind all the windows in the train, but most were outside. Trude gave me one hand and told me to walk a little faster. I asked her what we were going to do. She said, "Take a little walk and get something." I asked if my mother shouldn't come along. She said, "Let her rest awhile in the train. We'll bring some back for her." We passed some of the cars. People were sitting and lying outside the cars. Some had gone into the woods and were looking down from there. Trude took me with her, and we had to crawl over the rails, under the coupling between two cars. I asked if it wouldn't be dangerous if the train started moving, but Trude said the train wouldn't be moving as long as there was no locomotive.

We crossed a field. On that side of the train there weren't so many people. I saw some other people with wet faces and wet hands, but I couldn't see the water. Trude crouched down beside me with her face close to mine. She pointed her finger and said, "Look over there through the nettles, there's the water." I saw it. There was a path and the people were taking turns going for water. But Trude trampled the nettles flat and made a new path for us. She took an empty bottle out of a cloth she was carrying and filled it with water and put it down in the grass. Then she washed her face and her hands and told me to do the same. I washed my hands all right, but I left my face dry. Trude wet a corner of her cloth and wiped my cheeks and forehead. Then she started picking nettles. She said, "Give me a hand, then it'll go faster." But they stung me. She showed me how you have to grab the nettles from underneath, and then they don't sting. I couldn't do it. She tied her cloth around my hand. We raced to see who could pick the most. I won because I had the cloth on my hand. Then Trude tied the cloth around the nettles and took the bundle under her arm. I carried the bottle very carefully.

We crawled under the train again and the people asked how we'd gotten the water and the nettles. Trude said, "Picked them up there." We went back to the car where my mother was sitting.

My mother said she was glad we were back. Trude asked if she had a pot, but of course we didn't. I went out again with Trude. She went to another car, where somebody had made a little fire next to the tracks. She asked if she could use it. They said she could. There was a little pot next to the fire. Trude also asked if she could use the little pot. They said she could. She asked what had been in it. The man said, "The same." Trude put water in the pot. She held the pot as close as possible to the fire. When it got too hot she stepped back a little or changed hands. After a while the water started to boil. She put the pot down and put the nettles in. Then she let it boil some more. Now and then she put in more nettles. Then we took the soup to my mother. She drank some and said it was delicious vegetable soup. I drank a little too, but I didn't care for the nettles. Trude and my mother finished it up. Trude left the cloth and the rest of the nettles in the baggage net over my mother. She put the bottle of water on the floor next to my mother. We brought the pot back and sat by the fire for a while. Trude said, "This is better than the stinking train."

All of a sudden I heard shooting. The people screamed and ran out of the woods to the train. I told Trude we'd better get back in, but she said, "Take it easy, we will in a minute. There's no hurry." I looked along the train. A few people were still sitting outside, but most had gotten back in. I looked along the train in the other direction. Nobody was sitting there anymore. A

lot of people were standing outside the door of our car, waiting, some of them on the footboard. A little later, the last one
stepped in. Then I saw a soldier. He was carrying his gun
under his arm and he shot it off. But he kept coming slowly
along. There wasn't anybody behind him. He was coming
closer. I grabbed hold of Trude and tugged. I told her we should
get in or the soldier would shoot at us. She stood up slowly,
took me by the hand and walked slowly to the door of the car
where my mother was sitting. She said there was no hurry, but
of course I could get in if I was afraid.

At the door we stopped. Trude looked at the soldier. He was
right near us. I tugged at her hand because she had to help me
up to the lowest step. The soldier stopped beside us. Trude
looked at him. He looked at her. I looked into the hole of the
gun. I heard Trude saying there was no hurry. He said, "Get
in." Trude said there was nothing very remarkable about scar-
ing people when you had a gun, and he should look at the state
I was in. And she asked him what was the sense of getting into
the train when there was no locomotive. He said, "Just so you
get in before I come back. Tonight the doors are going to be
locked." He walked away. His gun swung around in our direction. I heard a shot. I tried to climb up on the footboard but I
fell down. "Do you think that's funny, you coward?" Trude
shouted. The soldier laughed. Up ahead of him the people
crowded into the train. The soldier looked around, raised his
gun up toward the woods, and fired. He laughed again. "The
damn fool," Trude said. She called out to my mother that
everything was all right and we'd stay outside a little longer.
Then she helped me up.

We went and sat under a tree. From there we could look
at the train and the meadow. The sky was full of colors because
the sun was setting.

The soldier came back and stood near us. He had his gun
over his shoulders and was holding his thumb through the
strap. He said, "You'll have to get in now."

We got up and went to the door. Trude stopped. She looked
at him and said, "Where are we? What's happening?" He
looked at her and said, "Where you are I can't tell you. But it's

all over." My hand hurt because Trude was holding it so tight. I looked up at her face. Then she picked me up and put me in the train. She got in too. Before pulling the door shut, she turned around to the soldier and said, "You rotten liar." He locked the door and walked slowly away.

Trude told me not to say anything about that conversation. My mother asked what had happened, and Trude said the soldier had wanted to frighten the people. But she didn't say anything about their squabble.

When it got dark, it was time for me to sleep. My mother said I couldn't sit on her lap because she kept having to go to the toilet. She said I could sleep in the baggage net over a different bench. I had a hard time getting in and then I was afraid I'd fall out if I turned over in my sleep. My mother arranged with the people for me to sleep on one of the benches. We'd all take turns sleeping on the bench. She let me have her turn.

I couldn't sleep and she let me get up again. It was dark. Now and then some planes passed over. I heard shots in the distance. The only other sound was people breathing in their sleep.

When it came my turn to lie down again, I still couldn't sleep. But the next time I was very tired. And there was nothing to see in the dark. So I just fell asleep.

SOLDIERS

They left me lying on the bench until I woke up by myself. It was light again. The train was still standing between the woods and the meadow. Through the window I saw the place where we had cooked the nettles. I went to my mother. I wanted to ask her if this was the morning after the night when I'd gone to sleep. My mother was sleeping. Trude was sitting with her. She said my mother was very tired and I should let her sleep. I went and sat on the bench. There was plenty of room. There weren't nearly so many people in our car. I asked Trude where all the people were. She said some were walking up and down in the train and others had gone to the hospital car. I went and stood by the window and looked out at the meadow. I heard marching. I heard footsteps on the roadbed. But I couldn't see anything.

The sound came closer. I pressed my nose to the window to see better. From the right side soldiers came marching in a row, and behind them more and more soldiers. I yelled to Trude that soldiers were coming. She said she knew it. I yelled that it was dangerous because there was a terrible lot of them. She stood up and looked through the window. "No," she said. "No," she said again. I yelled that she could see for herself. I could hear people yelling in the other cars. Trude grabbed my mother by the shoulder and shook her hard. Other people were looking out too. The first row of soldiers passed by. They were looking straight ahead. They were carrying their guns over their shoulders. In marching they stuck their legs out stiff. My mother turned her head to the wall and said, "Leave me alone." Trude started to cry. "Did you see that?" she asked.

"Did you see that? They're Russians. We're free. It's all over."
She hugged me. Other people started shouting that it was Russians and we were free. I started crying too. I told Trude it wasn't true, and they were ordinary soldiers same as in the camp and the soldier who'd chased us into the train the day before. "It's Russians, we're free," Trude said. She shook my mother again. My mother looked at her. Then she looked out of the window and hugged me. She held me tight and said, "Thank God." She also said that she felt sick and she'd better go quick to the hospital car, because otherwise we'd get sick too. She said I should stay with Trude and Trude should take good care of me. Trude promised she would, but she said it would probably be better for my mother to stay in our car until we could get out of the train because it was no good going to the hospital car and no need for it either.

I said it was ordinary soldiers and they'd all gone crazy. Trude showed me the difference between the krauts and the Russians. You could tell by their caps and their faces and their boots, but I couldn't see any difference. After a while another bunch of soldiers came by. Trude showed me that they had no guns and no helmets on their heads. Beside them were other soldiers with guns and caps. That was the Russians. The others were kraut prisoners. I kept looking. Now and then I'd call Trude and ask if the soldier I was pointing at was a Russian and the other a kraut prisoner. After the first few times I could tell.

The Russians took all the krauts away. All along the tracks there were krauts. I asked Trude if the Russians would shoot the krauts. She said she didn't think so, but she wouldn't mind if they did. Another child came and stood at my window. He had taken a branch from a tree and he pretended it was a gun. He shot at the krauts. I asked if I could shoot, too. He didn't want to let me, but Trude broke the branch in two and we both shot the kraut prisoners dead. Once in a while by mistake we hit a Russian a little.

There was a big noise in the train. People were screaming and crying, and children were shooting. Trude asked me why I'd

stopped shooting. I said we weren't really killing them. Then I
went to my mother and stroked her hand. She was asleep.

From where I was sitting I could see the soldiers' heads go
past. By then I knew the difference between the Russians and
the krauts.

There was still a lot of noise in the train. And it got very hot.
All morning the sun was coming down on the train. The windows couldn't be opened and the doors were still locked. By
that time there weren't so many soldiers passing. And they
were mostly Russians.

I heard a locomotive whistle. A little later we felt a jolt and
then we started moving. The people cheered.
    We stopped at a little station. Trude asked if I could read
what it was called. I read the word Tröbitz. She said I should
remember that well.
    We got out.
    My mother was taken to a hospital in a wagon.
    I went with Trude. We had to stand in line, but not for very
long. Then we went around to a lot of houses in Tröbitz with
some other people and a few Russian soldiers. We came to a
big white house. The Russians made them open up. Then the
people who lived there had to leave and we moved in. Trude
and me and another woman by the name of Eva had to go up
to the attic, because we climbed stairs best. There was a big
bed with plenty of room for us. Eva went out for a while and
came back with sheets and towels and soap. Trude washed me
and then herself all over with water and soap. Then I had to go
to bed. It was dark already. Trude said she'd sit with me until I
fell asleep. But then she'd have to go downstairs and maybe
outside. But in that case Eva would stay downstairs.
    The sheets were smooth and white and pulled good and
tight. There was a light-blue blanket over them. The bed was
big, I wouldn't fall out. And it was soft and warm. My head
was deep in the pillow.
    Trude drew the curtain. She let me have the light on.

I heard people walking around and laughing downstairs.

Trude came and sat on my bed. I asked her to put her hand on my forehead. My mother always did that because then I fell asleep quicker.

She put her hand on my head and said softly, "Our first night of freedom. Sleep tight."

POTATOES

A few days after we got to Tröbitz Trude and I were walking through the gray streets, past the gray houses. The houses had little windows, entirely different from at home. And shutters. There weren't many people in the street. It was lunchtime. The sun was shining. I was hot.

We came to a gate leading into a field. Trude opened it. She said it was allowed—she said anything we felt like doing was allowed—and closed it behind us.

"This way to the hospital is much shorter," she said. We walked on the grass. I had to be careful not to step in any cow flop.

We came to a farm. The barn was rigged up as a hospital. There was much more room than in the infirmary where my father had been. Here there was a gray-stone floor.

We went from bed to bed looking for my mother, but we didn't see her. We went back again and Trude asked someone who was sitting up in bed where my mother was.

"Her? Oh, she's sleeping," was the answer.

"Where is she?" Trude asked. "We've brought her some potatoes, and this is her son."

The woman wagged her head to one side. We turned around to another bed. Someone was lying there with the covers pulled up over her head. All you could see was a bunch of hair. Red hair. With lots of curls. Like my mother's hair.

Trude went over and lifted the blanket a little. She whispered to my mother that we were there and we very much wanted to talk to her and we'd brought her something. I went over to her bed too, but my mother pulled the blanket back over her head and lay still. She didn't say anything.

Trude turned around to the woman who had helped us and asked her how my mother was doing.

"Poorly," the woman answered. "She won't eat and she's very weak. And when she does eat something, she shits it right out. Or throws it up. Very bad. But she won't take any medicine, no matter what the doctor says. You'd better take your potatoes back with you."

Trude looked at my mother and told her again that we were there and we'd brought her some potatoes. She came over to me and pulled me a little way from the bed, past the foot end. She said I shouldn't go too near, because my mother was very sick and I could get sick too.

Then she took the bag with the potatoes in it and went over to the woman. I heard her say, "Then you take them. It would be a shame to take them back again because we have plenty. And if she won't eat them, they'll give you some pleasure at least."

The blanket on my mother's bed went up. Long curly red hair came out from under the raised blanket. And from under the blanket came screams.

"Don't let her have them. Don't. The bitch never gives anybody anything, so she shouldn't get anything. Give me those potatoes. They're mine. Give them here."

Trude went to my mother's bed and said she had already given the potatoes away. The woman stuffed the bag under her bed. The screaming went on.

"Why have you brought the child? You want him to die too? Everybody dies here, don't you know that?"

Trude said she should do what the doctor said and take her pills instead of screaming so.

She went away and came back with a cup of water.

"That's no drinking water. You want to kill me, don't you?" came the screams from the bed. Trude took a swallow herself and put the cup down by the bed. "And now take those pills."

The blanket was folded back on the bed. The hair was still sticking out in all directions and hanging down over her face.

"If I die, you'll be to blame," screamed the voice behind the hair. The pills disappeared into the mouth which I could hardly see, and the water was drunk.

"They're my potatoes. I want them back," she screamed.

Trude went over to the woman and spoke to her for a second. She promised to bring her different potatoes. The woman shrugged her shoulders and said, "She's crazy." I called out to Trude that the bag was under the bed. She grabbed it and put it on the other bed. The person in the other bed grabbed the bag and looked in. Her hand went into the bag and came out with a potato. She looked at the potato. She emptied out the bag on the bed. She raised the hand with the potato in it and held it back near the wall. The woman who had helped us yelled, "Watch out" and grabbed her pillow. The potato hit her square in the face. Trude screamed, "Have you gone crazy?" The woman threw her pillow at the potato thrower and began to cry. The potatoes flew thick and fast. One of them hit Trude. She yelled to me to duck or run away. A scream went with each flying potato, "You're trying to kill me"; "I'll show you"; "That rotten bitch, she's the crazy one."

Two men came running in. They took away the rest of the potatoes and made my mother lie down. One of them gave her an injection. They held her still for a little while. Then they put the blankets back over her and took the pillow back to the other bed. They told us we'd have to leave.

Trude took me by the hand and we went over to the bed. She was lying on her side with her back to the other woman. We went to the side of the bed where her face was. The men had smoothed her hair back. Now I recognized my mother's face. She laughed a little and said she was glad to see me; she said I was looking well and I should be careful not to get sick. She began to cry.

Trude pulled the blanket up over her shoulder and said she'd take good care of me.

"You must do what the doctor says, then you'll soon be back with us again," she said.

My mother fell asleep. We went away.

A few days later we went for a walk outside the village and picked flowers for our room. They were white and yellow.

Trude said they were daisies. I had to pick them way down, close to the ground, or else the stem would be too short to be put in a glass. There was just the two of us. All I could hear now and then was a cow or a bird or the wind blowing in my ears. I was hot.

I asked Trude if we could visit my mother again soon. She said, "No, we can't; the road is closed." I said the last time she had simply opened the gate. She said, "That's not possible anymore." I said there was a different way to the hospital, not across the field but through the village. Even if it was longer, I said, we could go that way. She began to cry and said, "I've told you the road is closed. All the roads are closed. That one too." I asked her how all the roads could be closed when we went there only a few days ago. She said, "That's the way it is." She had stopped crying. "I'll explain later."

I asked if I could go and see my mother when the roads were opened up again. She said, "Later.

"Should we pick a few more flowers?" Trude asked.

We picked a nice bunch of flowers for our room.

SLAUGHTERING

Trude had gone upstairs to attend to our flowers. In the garden behind our house some men were chasing a pig. They were trying to catch it, but it kept getting away. They called out to each other and clapped their hands to drive the pig back. The pig was screeching. Some women at the windows were screeching. I stood by the door. Two men caught the pig. One held him by the ears and the other by the tail. It squealed and squealed. The other men came closer to the pig. One had a knife in his hand. The men dragged the pig by the feet. It fell to the ground. The man with the knife raised his arm high up and shouted to the others to stand aside. Then he stuck the pig hard with the knife. Blood squirted in all directions. Some of the men looked away. The squealing got fainter. The man stuck again and then again. A woman ran out. She had a knife in her hand too. She ran to the pig and cut off a chunk. The women at the windows cheered. Some of the others ran out with knives and cut off chunks. They took the chunks back in with them. There was blood all over. Somebody said it was forbidden to eat pig meat.

Eva came out and asked what all the noise was about. She looked at the pig and she looked at the people who were cutting off chunks. She came over to me and took me by the hand. She pulled me inside with her.

"Where's Trude?" she asked. "What are you doing out here all alone with these crazy people?" I said we'd picked flowers and Trude had gone upstairs to put them in our room. Eva went through the hallway with me, opened the front door, and pulled me outside. It was much quieter in front of the house, though you could still hear the screeching in the back garden. There was a bench against the wall near the door. We sat down.

"You must be very unhappy about what's happened," Eva said. I said I could stand it, because I wasn't a baby anymore. She said, "But it's very sad for you." I said the squealing had been awful. I told her the men had had a lot of trouble and that blood had splashed all over them and everything was full of the pig's blood. Eva asked, "Do you mind that more?" I kicked at the gravel and watched the pebbles flying through the air.

She asked, "Don't you know about your mother?"

I kicked some more pebbles and said yes, I knew the road was closed. She said, "Yes." I looked at her mouth. "And that makes you very sad, doesn't it?" I said yes, of course it was bad, but I'd be able to go and see my mother later.

"Later? What do you mean by later?"

I told her Trude had told me the road was closed, but I'd be able to go and see my mother later. I said I didn't understand, but Trude would explain it to me later.

Eva stood up and grabbed me by the hand. She pulled me into the house and up the stairs. All the while she kept saying, "It looks like they've all gone crazy around here. Later. Later."

We got to the top and Eva threw the door of our room open without knocking. Trude wouldn't like that.

Trude had been looking out of the window. The daisies were in three glasses on white table covers. The beds were made and the white sheets were pulled tight over the top part of the blankets and a little over the white pillows. Yellow light was coming in through the white curtains.

She screamed at Trude, "Have you gone completely crazy too? The child doesn't even know about his mother. He expects to go and see her later. What kind of lunacy is that?"

Trude said, "Don't scream so. He knows. He knows perfectly well. I told him all about it."

Eva said to me, "What did she tell you? Something about a road being closed?"

I nodded. Trude said, "You see?" Eva said to me, "And that

you'd be able to go and see your mother later?" I nodded. She looked at Trude. Trude said softly, "Oh, that will come."

Eva took hold of me. She planted herself in front of me. Then she squatted down on her heels. She said, "Listen, angel. I've got to tell you something very bad." I looked at Trude, but she was looking out of the window. I looked at Eva's mouth. "Very bad, do you hear? Very, very bad." She spoke very slowly as if I didn't know Dutch, and very loud and clear.

"You can't go and see your mother ever again. Never again. Your mother is dead."

I said that was nonsense because Trude had only said the road was closed and I could go and see her later. I looked at Trude.

Eva said, "She's dead. You know what that means. Dead like your father. So you can't go and see her anymore. Do you understand?"

I said Trude had told me I could go and see her later.

Eva said, "Just ask Trude. Trude, is his mother dead?" She asked her for me.

Trude turned her head a little in our direction, but she kept looking out of the window. Very softly she said, "Yes."

"And will he be able to go and see his mother later?" Eva asked Trude. She put her hand on the back of my neck and turned my head toward Trude.

"Oh, I meant something different," Trude said.

"Will he be able to go and see her?" Eva screamed. Trude looked at her and at me. She turned around and let the curtain go. It fell back in front of the window.

"No," she said. "You won't. Your mother is dead."

Eva stood up. She said, "It's terrible. But you had to know."

I nodded. There was a table in front of me. On the cloth there was a glass with flowers in it. I picked up the glass and threw it on the floor. I stamped on the flowers and pulled the cloth off the table. I hit the glass with it. I pushed the table over and kicked at it. I screamed at Trude, I called her a bitch and said I wasn't a baby anymore. I trembled and started to cry. I said they were rotten flowers and that she herself had closed the road and given away my mother's potatoes and given my mother pills and bad water and it was her fault she was dead and I couldn't go and see her anymore. I was hot. I tried to say even more but I couldn't. I fell down. I noticed that Eva caught me. She and Trude tried to lay me on the bed. I told Trude to go away and leave me alone because she'd lied to me and I'd never believe her again. Trude went a few steps away. She stayed in the room, but I couldn't say another word. Eva undressed me and put me to bed.

She gave me a kiss on the forehead.

My skin was burning but I couldn't push the covers off.

"He's got a fever. We'll have to get the doctor," Eva said.

SICKNESS

"Trude, come. He's fallen out of bed."

I was lifted up and put down on the bed. I felt a hand on my forehead.

"It's gone down." I opened my eyes. There was too much light and I closed them again in a hurry.

They called my name. I tried to open my eyes again. I wanted to put my hand over my eyes to keep out the light. But I couldn't move my hands. I wanted to say it was too light and I wanted to ask why they hadn't woken me sooner, but I couldn't.

"He's saying something. Can you understand him?"

They called my name again. I nodded.

"He understands. Oh, Trude, he understands. Thank God, then the worst is over."

I woke up. Trude was sitting beside me on a chair. Eva was standing at the foot of the bed, looking at me. It was gray outside. Inside, a candle was burning.

"My, have you slept." They laughed. I said I hadn't slept well.

"That's because you had a high fever." They said I had screamed and thrown the covers off and thrashed around like a crazy man and fallen on the floor. And that they had kept putting washcloths on my forehead. And the doctor had come.

"Can you remember all that?"

I said I remembered that they had put me to bed and that the light was too bright and that I had dreamed.

They asked me what I had dreamed. I said something about snow and fire, and that was all I knew.

I asked if I could get up or if it was too early and why they were dressed. They said it was evening and not morning and that I had to stay in bed till I was better.

I said I hadn't been sick at all, I'd only had crazy dreams.

Trude said the doctor was coming soon and I was really sick with a fever and I had to stay in bed. I asked how it could be evening when I'd gone to bed in the evening. Trude said, "Because you've been sick for five days and you've had a terrible fever." I looked at Eva and said that was impossible, because I'd gone to bed in the evening and I'd certainly know it if I'd been in bed for five days. Eva said Trude was right and they'd been afraid I would die, but it was over now.

"Now you must eat well and get strong again."

I could tell I had a fever. But I didn't believe the five days. There was a dark hole in the time.

AMSTERDAM

We were sitting up high in an open truck. The front of the platform was full of stuff: suitcases, duffel bags, rags and blankets. Trude had liberated a sea bag. I was sitting high up, looking down on the people who were sitting on the floor of the platform. There were benches along the side walls. Trude was sitting on one of them. She shouted at me to button my coat up tight. She had piled up some bundles around my legs to keep the wind off. Someone yelled, "A hundred kilometers more."

A woman crawled up to the driver's cab and banged her fist on the roof. A head came around the corner. A Canadian climbed onto our platform. He put his ear close to the woman's mouth and put one arm over her shoulder. They nodded and shook their heads. They said "fast" and "slow" and "okay." The Canadian handed out cigarettes and chocolate and climbed back again over the edge of the platform into the cab. I didn't want any chocolate. The engine roared louder than ever. The woman banged on the cab again. The trees whished by even faster. "Sixty kilometers more."

I had to make peepee. I shouted to Trude that I had to. I shouted again and then another time. She crawled over to me. She asked me if I wanted to do it over the side of the truck. I said no, I didn't. In that case, she said, I'd have to hold it in. I said I couldn't hold it anymore. She said then I'd just have to do it in my pants. I cried and said my mother never let me do that. She said I could do it now, just this once, and my mother would certainly have said the same thing. I didn't believe her.

She said then I'd just have to do it over the side. I asked her to take the heavy bundle off my lap. She started to push it away, but I said it was too late. She left it where it was.

Slowly my pants got warm and wet. I sighed and shivered and let the peepee flow. For a second it was very still. No more wind, no more engine noise, no more people yelling. I saw the soft bundle on my lap. I felt my legs and belly getting warm and wet. I wished my whole body could be as warm and wet.

"Forty kilometers more."

I was cold. A few people started singing. The people were leaning out over both sides as far as possible. They yelled, "There's another one. There comes another one. Can you read it?"

"Only sixteen kilometers more. We're almost there."

A lot of the people started crying and hugging each other.

"Now nothing can happen to us. We're there."

"Don't rejoice too soon," said one man.

"Fourteen, only fourteen kilometers." I heard cheering and clapping from the other trucks. First from the ones ahead of us, then from the ones behind us.

We slowed down.

"Amsterdam, six kilometers."

"I see the houses."

"So do I."

Suddenly everybody fell down. We had picked up speed. The Canadian looked around the corner. "Okay?"

The people who had fallen shouted, "Okay." Their faces were laughing and angry. They didn't get up.

"We're there. We're home."

"We're back."

"Hurrah for Amsterdam."

The people hugged each other and wished each other luck. Me too. The truck was bumping along. The people crawled around the platform, fell down, stood up again.

———

Some of the people climbed over the side before we even stopped. They dropped on the ground and kissed the stones. They cried.

Trude took me into a building. We went to a big room. There were straw mattresses on the floor, with blankets on them.

Trude washed me all over with soap, and they gave me different clothes.

Then we celebrated. I didn't have to go to bed right away.

Later Trude put me to bed. She said she was going back to the celebration. That was all right with me.

"Sweet dreams. Your first night back in Amsterdam." She kissed me and went away. At the door she turned around again and laughed.

It was still in the room. From the celebration I could hear music and singing and happy screams.

AUNT LISA

Trude found out that Mr. Paul had offered to take care of me. We went to see Mr. Paul and his wife a few times. Mr. Paul's wife said I should call her Aunt Lisa instead of Mrs. G.

She wasn't my aunt at all.

Trude said she had to go away for a while and I could stay with Mrs. G. I said I'd rather not. She took me there.

Trude was back from her trip. She came to tea. Mrs. G. asked her, "How are you getting along?"

"All right."

Mrs. G. told her I was going to school again. She said I'd started calling her Aunt Lisa and I didn't eat enough.

Trude and Mrs. G. were in the living room. They were sitting quietly in their chairs, each with a cup of tea. I was standing on the brown wooden floor in the hallway. The living room door was open, the other doors were closed. The hallway was dark and cold. Trude and Mrs. G. were looking out. They didn't move. They didn't speak. I held my breath and listened to see if they were still breathing.

Trude said my not eating much wasn't so bad, she said it would change. She said I hadn't eaten much in the camp either.

Mrs. G. said, "If he doesn't eat well, he'll die. He's got to eat."

Trude said there was nothing she could do about it and she had to be going. I started crying.

At supper I didn't eat anything. Aunt Lisa made me take my plate to the bedroom. After a while she came in. She wanted to feed me. She asked me why I wouldn't eat anything. I said I wasn't hungry and it was too much for me. She said I had to finish my supper. "You're almost eight. You're not a baby anymore."

I took a bite and I almost had to throw up. I said it was too hot in the bedroom. Aunt Lisa hugged me gently and asked why I had cried so that afternoon. She brought a spoonful of food up to my mouth. I turned my head to one side. She put the spoon down, took my head gently in her hands, shook her head and said, "You've got to eat something. If you don't, you'll die. And we want to keep you with us."

She pulled my head toward her and kissed me on the lips.

My legs trembled. My hands grabbed the plate and threw it on the floor. I stamped on it, I burst out crying and I screamed: "You kissed me on the lips. Now I'll die. My mother told me so herself."

My mouth filled with vomit. I almost suffocated. It came splashing out on the floor. It spattered her legs. She said, "Now look what you've done. Just clean it up. You're not a baby anymore."

She gave me a cloth. I started wiping it up.

Afterword

Jona Oberski's *Childhood* begins with a voice in the dark, reassuring us, and then transitions to the extreme proximity of a child's focus, a focus that is all the more intense because the child is undergoing an anxiety-producing change:

> "Don't be afraid. Everything's all right. I'm right here."
> The hand on my cheek was my mother's; her face was close to mine. I could hardly see her. She whispered and stroked my hair. It was dark. The walls were wood. There was a funny smell. It sounded like there were other people there. My mother lifted my head up and pushed her arm under it. She hugged me and kissed me on the cheek.
> I asked her where my father was.

Childhood is a fictionalized account of Oberski's experiences in the Bergen-Belsen concentration camp from when he was four to seven years old. The novel was first published in Dutch as *Kinderjaren* in 1978, and is a laconic little book—my edition, with fairly large print and wide margins, runs to only 116 pages—that was acclaimed throughout Europe as a small masterpiece, and subsequently translated around the world. The author produced two more literary works in Dutch, *The Uninvited Visitor* and *The Proprietor of No Man's Land*, but otherwise published in the field in which he made his living: nuclear and particle physics.

And there's a scientist's logic to the lucidity and elegance of the book's design. Nearly all of its aesthetic strategies are on display in its opening three paragraphs, quoted above. We begin with a child's vague apprehension of an adult's fearful reassurances, and progress to his determination to focus on the sensory here and now as a way of controlling his terror and negotiating his world (*Okay, that's mom's hand, touching me, and she's right nearby*); to the usefulness of such a strategy as a way of orienting one's self (*it's dark, the walls are wood, and it sounds like there are other people here*); to the limitations of his ability to articulate, and the way he makes use of those limitations to protect his own psyche from devastating information (*"There was a funny smell"*); and finally to how, despite all of that, he continues to pursue information (*Okay, great: you're still here, and you still love me. Now: where's Dad?*).

One of the pleasures that fiction can deliver is, of course, the godlike ability to flit from sensibility to sensibility—to penetrate *everyone's* minds, and to know with certainty what everyone is thinking: a mobility and omniscience that we never get to experience in our regular lives. Another pleasure that fiction can offer, though, is the opportunity to inhabit a single, other sensibility, as limited as (or perhaps even more limited than) our own, as fully as possible. Both pleasures are exercises in the empathetic imagination, but for me the latter option nearly always seems, when done well, more bracingly revelatory as a crash course in empathy. And I tend to believe that most of us need as bracingly revelatory a crash course in empathy as we can get.

A commonplace claim about the relationship between the Holocaust and the arts has been that the enormity of the suffering generated by such an extreme event must defeat any attempt at adequate representation. *Childhood*'s design seems to attack that problem head-on by foregrounding its narrator's handicaps as a narrator. By making *such* a small child our guide to that infernal region, the book at once enacts any number of ways in which the implacable and impossible fact of the Holocaust makes children of us all: the inherent powerlessness of the child's position; the inherent limitations of the child's ability to articulate suffering; the inherent limitations of the child's ability to fully *connect* to suffering; and the inherent impossibility of testifying for others, or ever testifying for all.

There's an understandable impulse on the part of artists facing such a daunting, if not impossible, task to stage a kind of mastery of the material. A film like Steven Spielberg's *Schindler's List* owes much of its critical and commercial success to the smooth efficiency with which it familiarizes its audience with an introductory smattering of the more hellish events of the Holocaust: a kind of greatest hits of the varieties of horror stories that emerged from eyewitness accounts. At one point during the liquidation of the Krakow ghetto, we find ourselves on a bluff above the city with Oskar Schindler, and are allowed to view an actual panorama of nightmarish atrocities taking place, a cinematic version of the oddly homey sprawl one might encounter in a painting by Brueghel or Bosch: over in this corner, they're lining up Jews six deep to see how many one rifle shot will penetrate; over in that corner, they're making a husband watch while they shoot his wife in the head.

And there certainly are horrors that are obliquely and not-so-obliquely depicted throughout the short span of *Childhood*. But partially because of its choice of narrator, *Childhood* does not take the form of a catalog of horrors; it renders instead its narrator's both natural and willful inclination to focus on what *he* wishes to focus on, and the effect is both saving and unsettling. At times, in the face of trauma, the focus could not be more microcosmic, prioritizing completely a child's frame of reference:

> Somebody shouted shhh. My mother whispered so close to my ear that it tickled. "Go to sleep now. I'm right here, I won't go away. Tomorrow we'll take a look at our camp, and in a few days we'll go home to Daddy."
>
> She gave me a kiss. The air in my nose was cold. It was cold under the blankets too. I cuddled up to my mother and her warm breath blew into my nose.

That determined worm's-eye view allows the narrator to continually access his sense of wonder, and of what the world has to offer:

The rain was coming down on my hood. My hands under my cape kept dry. I put one hand through the slit. I saw the raindrops coming down on my hand. The drops kept giving me little cold taps, each time in a different place.

One of the subjects with which nearly all Holocaust texts grapple is the issue of the victims' compliance with the Nazis' genocidal project: the way the victims were over and over again apparently unable to take on agency on their own behalf. For all sorts of reasons that seem to us both explicable and inexplicable, those victims appeared at times to continue to play their role in a kind of dreamlike state, perhaps hoping for the best while they continued to observe, sometimes impassively, both others' and their own destruction.

For a boy as young as *Childhood*'s narrator, how or why he got here is beside the point. He has ended up here, and now he has to deal with it. Sometimes that means acquiring knowledge, and much of the book's power, as we might expect, derives from its juxtaposition of the narrator's heartbreaking innocence with what needs to be learned. Early on in their time in the camp the narrator's mother sends him, despite his protests, off with some other children to carry the giant cooking pots back to the kitchen, where the camp worker in charge tells them all to clean out the pots, meaning he gives them permission to finish what's left in them, at which point all the children except the narrator lean into them so fully that some can't keep their feet on the ground. The narrator, baffled, does nothing, and when they're all about to leave, the camp worker asks if what they'd been doing tasted good, and everyone else shouts "yes." Once the narrator is back with his mother she's horrified to learn that he missed his chance at additional nutrition. Now, he'll have to wait a whole week for another chance, which leaves him with only the poignant knowledge of what he lost:

Every day after lunch, a little while after the pots had been taken away, I could hear a loud "yes" from the kitchen shack on the other side. I stood by the fence with the other children and listened. I'd heard that sound before, but I'd never known what it was.

Sometimes the book's strategy is to let its narrator report to us information that he doesn't fully understand but we do, because of our greater frame of reference:

The door opened. Everybody stopped talking. Some more people came into the room. Most of them had long black coats on.

And sometimes he knows *and* doesn't know. Having been bullied by a shopkeeper's son for having been a Jew, he seems to have understood nothing until he finds his mother inside the shop and she asks if he left his toys—a bucket, a spade, and a mold for making sand pies—outside, at which point his circumspection makes clear that on some level he *has* understood what went on:

She went and got them. I didn't want to go with her. I looked out of the window. She came back. I ran to the door to meet her and asked if she had the mold too. She went back, but she couldn't find the mold.

What seems at times like diffidence reveals itself on a second reading to resemble something more like comprehension. Later on, we're told:

My mother had sewn a yellow star on my coat. She said, "Look, now you've got a pretty star, just like Daddy." I thought the star was pretty, but I'd rather have gone without.

And at times he just lets slip that he knows and feels more than he's letting on:

In the evening there was talk and people said nobody'd be going to Palestine. But somebody said, "Shh, there are children here."

I pretended their talking didn't bother me. And after a while I
really didn't hear it anymore.

That last sentence actually allows us to glimpse the mechan-
ism of repression in operation. Knowledge is filtered in, and
buried. A compromised innocence is restored.

Knowing and not knowing, some power and total powerlessness, complicity and innocence: even in a narrator such as
this, the categories are muddied, and the lack of clarity seems
crucial to the subject's ability to hold his psyche together.

Avoidance in general works to get our narrator through.
Another way in which he deals with his new situation is by not
dwelling on the choices that he and his parents have made in
order to arrive at the camps, and also by not dwelling on the
operations of chance. Choice and/or the vagaries of chance:
the sort of factors, in other words, that form the *heart* of a
traditional dramatic narrative and which allow a text like
Schindler's List, despite all the horror that it chronicles, to
deliver so much satisfaction to its audience.

There's another quietly subversive effect to employing such a
young narrator, and in doing so with such restraint: it allows
the book to unobtrusively stage him as a startlingly impassive
witness to his own family's tragedy. He's beginning to grasp
the simple secret of his new universe: he could be killed any-
where, anytime. That understanding, combined with his
increasing rage at his own powerlessness, creates in him a
growing detachment about his own and his loved ones' safety:
on a dare, he sticks his tongue out at an armed German guard;
and later, having found himself apparently locked into the
morgue, he takes the opportunity to root around the jumble of
bodies.

According to the Russian poet Nadezhda Mandelstam,
under terror there seems to be no leisure for ordinary heart-
breaks. And yet part of what's radical about *Childhood* is the
way it models the narrator's experience of Bergen-Belsen as an
echo of psychoanalysts' view of the way we watch movies in a
theater. Our narrator models for us that dreamlike receptivity,
that temporarily regressive state that's like hypnosis, which

allows him to merge with what he's watching. On the one hand, he finds himself in a state of enforced passivity. And on the other, he has stopped turning away. He's beside himself, watching himself. And so he feels not quite responsible. That denial has, again, an obvious usefulness.

Making Oskar Schindler the protagonist of your Holocaust narrative allows you to foreground the heroic, and the uplifting. That's because in the face of so much iniquity, Oskar *acts* on behalf of others, and does so with decisive success, even in a situation in which the odds are overwhelmingly against him. Like all of our culture's heroes in disguise—individuals who at first didn't appear to be exceptional but then stepped forward and were forged into something noble by the crucible of extreme events—he knows what to do, and he does it.

That is not the way *Childhood* works. It continues to refuse to provide us with much by way of dramatic event in this, perhaps the most dramatic of historical circumstances, and it makes us wait for long stretches while our narrator just observes. Sometimes he seems moved; sometimes he seems frightened; sometimes he seems bored; sometimes he has to work to figure out what's going on. Does his position sound familiar? It should.

Childhood presents us with a child struck dumb and unthinking by the incalculable disaster that's broken over his head—so much so that, despite his love for his parents, there are many moments in which he is an unmoved bystander to their suffering, as though he were an old dog noting a far-off traffic accident.

His self-preserving focus is so intent on finding those pockets of respite wherever he can that, informed by someone at the infirmary that his father is failing fast and that his mother needs to come right away if she wants to see him alive for one last time, he becomes absorbed in a private game on the way to tell his mother, and forgets entirely to deliver his message.

One of the most devastating scenes in the book occurs after the narrator's mother has arranged through bribes a private rendezvous with her husband, smuggled in from the man's side of the camp. She's brought the narrator along and has told him only to expect a surprise, and after he gets over his shock at his father's transformation, he registers his mother's desperate need to connect, perhaps for one last time:

> They walked around the room together, talking. My mother whispered something and hugged my father. He said, "Oh no, we can't do that." "Why not?" said my mother. "I know how much you want to, it'll be all right." "But what about the child?" my father asked. "He won't notice," my mother said. But he said it wouldn't do. "Then he'll just have to wait outside," my mother said. And she came over to me and told me to say good-bye to my father, and then to wait in the corridor until she came out. I didn't want to. My father said, "Let him stay. We don't really have to." My mother said to me, "You do as you're told," and took me out of the room.

But the narrator's not sitting still for that. He tries to go back into the room and is stopped by the guard who arranged the meeting, and he starts crying and screaming and banging on their door. Does he know he's risking all of their lives? He doesn't say. And the answer is: yes and no.

His mother comes out to quiet him down. His father shouts for her to bring him in with them, and then tells him that he can stay but that he can't look at them. Of course, he does anyway:

> "It's no good," my father said. "Anyway, it's almost time. It's no good in such a hurry."
> The man knocked and called out, "Five minutes more." My mother turned around and pulled her coat tight. She came over to me and took me by the hand. She pulled me through the door and told the man to let me out and not let me back in, even if I cried. She said to me, "I won't be long. Wait outside and don't cry or I never want to see you again." She left me there and went into the room. The man looked out through a little hole, opened the door and pushed me out. I sat down on the wooden steps and waited.

Does he know what he's done? Yes. Does he care? Here's how the section ends:

The next day was my birthday. I asked if there was a cake for me too. My mother said she'd used everything up for my father. This time I wouldn't get anything, but the next time I'd get whatever I wanted. I wanted a new jumping jack and a dump truck and to steer the ferry myself.

There's still compassion in this world, but it's approached with such wariness, and treated so much as the mysterious and near-miraculous condition that it must be in such a place, that we're always aware that its appearance must be momentary and evanescent. As even his parents have taught him, in a world in which survival is the priority, privilege keeps its head down and hurries about its business. When the family believes that they're among the lucky Jews who are going to be pulled from the group and released to Palestine, their leave-taking is narrated as follows:

When we left the field, the people shook hands with us and patted my father on the back. They said, "Good luck" and patted me on the head. My father and mother just sighed. I asked my father why he didn't look at the people when they spoke to us. I always had to look at anyone who spoke to me. My mother said she'd explain later, now we had to hurry. A lot of people went back to their shacks. Some were crying.

As mentioned before, part of what contributes to the narrator's emotional cossetedness is his rage at his situation, a rage that's most vividly on display in his responses to his mother's upset at his risk-taking, such as when he searches for his father's body in the "dreadhouse," the morgue, on a dare from the other children:

She asked what the dreadhouse was. I said she must know, it was the place where they put the bodies, and she must know, too, that they'd chucked my father in there, and she must know, too, that he didn't even have a sheet. I told the other children he had one, though I'd seen him myself without a sheet. And I screamed that she must be crazy to let them chuck him in there without a sheet, and she hadn't even told me they'd taken him out of the infirmary because then I could have gone and said good-bye to him, and I thought it was disgusting and it was her fault if he was in there all naked with the bodies. My mother only said, "No" and "It's not true," but I didn't listen and I said there was no point in lying to me because I'd seen it with my own eyes.

We note—speaking of that rage—the extra brutality of his choice of the verb "chucked." And we note too how much his response makes clear that he understands just how much all of this knowing and not knowing has been a function of volition, and *not* innocence. As the book proceeds, our narrator records; he endures; he goes about the business of pulling what pleasure he can from the life he's been given. He's a witness, to be sure, but not one who allows us to feel that there's something particularly heroic about the act.

There is, in fact, a famous literary antecedent of *active* witnessing, when it comes to Holocaust texts, and by another victim of Bergen-Belsen: Anne Frank's *Diary of a Young Girl*. Her book became a fixture in high school and middle school lesson plans precisely because her fierce desire to work through the implications of what was happening to her *turned* her enforced passivity into something heroic. Faced with her situation, she did her best to work through what she could, ethically, philosophically, and metaphysically. Other less well-known memoirs and diaries from young people—*The Diary of Dawid Rubinowicz*, or *The Diary of Dawid Sierakowiak*, for example—have operated the same way.

Does our narrator? He can't. Or won't. Where he ends up, philosophically and emotionally, pretty much eliminates him from middle school reading lists.

He knows—or believes—that it's *never* been his life to control. And so, except for the occasional rageful lashing out, he's never acted as though it was. Change in *Childhood* just keeps on occurring, seemingly under no one's control. And the camp's effect of *eroding* his sense of what's possible, by way of autonomous action—and its only-partial restoration, once he's freed from the camp—are central to what makes the book so stark.

It's generally agreed that in the face of the Holocaust, the role of art seems to be primarily to provide testimony. But if the impulse behind that testimony has to be to tell the truth, the whole truth and nothing but the truth—if, in other words, the extremity of the subject creates a special urgency about the need to be comprehensive—then we should remember that that oath in a fiction not only makes the work more susceptible to perjury: it almost guarantees it. Making a small child our guide foregrounds how inadequate and incomplete our apprehension must be. In fact, our incomplete understanding and the need to improve it is deftly modeled for us in a scene in which the narrator's mother realizes that she has to surreptitiously teach him about the lethal ubiquity of the camp's watchtowers, after he thinks he's gotten away with sticking his tongue out at a guard, just because the guard who was mocked didn't notice:

> "Now listen carefully," my mother said. "I'm going to show you something without using my finger. And you mustn't point either. And you mustn't look that way too long. Just do exactly as I say. Look over my shoulder. Do you see the watchtower?"
>
> All I could see was the shacks and behind them some tall poles. I told her so. "And what do you see on top of those poles?" she asked. I looked a little higher and I saw some kind of a hut. I told her so.
>
> "That hut is the watchtower. There's a watchtower on every side of the camp. Didn't you know that?"

The narrator explains that he hadn't, and, while he watches, one of the guards turns in his direction, and points his gun at him.

And thus our narrator also foregrounds for us what must finally constitute our lack of comprehension. As many have pointed out before, much of what the Nazis did and what occurred falls into the category of the unbelievable. We learn, for example, in Alain Resnais' documentary *Night and Fog* that the ceiling of the gas chamber at Auschwitz—the concrete ceiling—was *torn into* by human fingernails, so great were the death agonies of the victims. Could we *believe* this if the camera didn't show us the marks? In foregrounding our incredulity, our narrator also foregrounds the lack of a shared viewpoint in the face of such a radical event, since, as commentators from Raul Hilberg on have pointed out, witnesses to the Holocaust fall into three rough categories—perpetrators, bystanders, and victims—whose differences are so radical that they go beyond a diversity of point of view, to something like an incommensurability of perception.

Finally, our narrator, in his indefatigable desire to *view* what's happening—as when he searches through the pile of corpses in the dreadhouse, seeking his father—reminds us of the potential ethical implications of our own desires, when it comes to these sorts of texts. Perhaps the biggest problem confronting anyone trying to construct a piece of art about the Holocaust involves the awful disparity between the human agony at its center and the pleasures one necessarily derives from aesthetic works. Since eliminating such pleasure is impossible by definition in a successful work of art, all one can do, one would think, is to make the work self-conscious, at least, about that tension.

Engaging representations of extreme suffering entail both educating one's self in empathy *and* taking on a certain detachment. That detachment links the viewer or reader, disturbingly enough, to the Holocaust's original spectators: the bystanders, and to an even greater extent, the perpetrators. As many have pointed out, nearly all of the documentary images of the Holocaust that exist were generated by the Nazis themselves, so that they could apparently re-view, and reconsider, the destruction of the Jews at a later date. That famous photo from the Warsaw Ghetto of the young boy with his hands in the air, standing in front of a group of mostly women and children—probably the single most iconic image of the Holocaust—comes from SS Major General Jürgen Stroop's report to his superiors on the liquidation of the ghetto. (The photo is captioned

"Pulled from the bunkers by force.") And what the Nazi photographer who served under him captured, for all time, is beautifully articulated in David Roskies' analysis of the image in his book *Against the Apocalypse*:

> Everyone is carrying something, as if, at this late date, there were still somewhere to go. And then the eye fixes on the child, so neatly dressed, so bewildered. Whose child is he? It doesn't matter, because they will all eventually perish. Yet the child alone is surely all of us, the adult made a child by the Holocaust that no one can explain to us. And the child is alone, too, because no one seems to be coming after him—or is even concerned that he keeps his hands up; he couldn't do anything with his hands down, anyway. He seems, then, to be at once imitating the adults and volunteering himself as one.

Here's our narrator at the book's end, with both his parents gone and his life devastated, attempting the same thing, while peering into a nearby room at one woman who brought him out of the camp and another who has volunteered to adopt him:

> Trude and Mrs. G. were in the living room. They were sitting quietly in their chairs, each with a cup of tea. I was standing on the brown wooden floor in the hallway. The living room door was open, the other doors were closed. The hallway was dark and cold. Trude and Mrs. G. were looking out. They didn't move. They didn't speak. I held my breath and listened to see if they were still breathing.

I love, in that last line, the eloquence of the tentative and incremental nature of his expectations. He's standing by, ready to go back to pretending that a version of the life that he once knew can still continue. If it's a heroism at all that he's practicing, it's the most quotidian kind of heroism, the kind that goes unnoticed by history, and the kind that may register on only the sorts of scales available to the arts.

JIM SHEPARD